"Can we talk, Milla?"

"Talk about what?" Her voice waffled, and she hoped he hadn't noticed.

"About you and me."

His gaze snagged hers, and even though sexual awareness nearly knocked her for a loop, getting involved with him wasn't a good idea.

The problem was her mind had no trouble believing that, but her body wasn't listening.

She turned, trying to break eye contact with the man who aroused everything but her common sense. "Nothing has changed."

But that couldn't be further from the truth.

Things had changed, big-time. Kyle just didn't know it yet.

Dear Reader,

Well, if it's true that March comes in like a lion and goes out like a lamb, you're going to need some fabulous romantic reads to get you through the remaining cold winter nights. Might we suggest starting with a new miniseries by bestselling author Sherryl Woods? In *Isn't It Rich?*, the first of three books in Ms. Wood's new MILLION DOLLAR DESTINIES series, we meet Richard Carlton, one of three brothers given untold wealth from his aunt Destiny. But in pushing him toward beautiful—if klutzy—PR executive Melanie Hart, Aunt Destiny provides him with riches that even money can't buy!

In *Bluegrass Baby* by Judy Duarte, the next installment in our MERLYN COUNTY MIDWIVES miniseries, a handsome but commitment-shy pediatrician shares a night of passion with a down-to-earth midwife. But what will he do when he learns there might be a baby on the way? Karen Rose Smith continues the LOGAN'S LEGACY miniseries with *Take a Chance on Me*, in which a sexy, single CEO finds the twin sister he never knew he had—and in the process is reunited with the only woman he ever loved. In *Where You Least Expect It* by Tori Carrington, a fugitive accused of a crime he didn't commit decides to put down roots and dare to dream of the love, life and family he thought he'd never have. Arlene James wraps up her miniseries THE RICHEST GALS IN TEXAS with *Tycoon Meets Texan!* in which a handsome billionaire who can have any woman he wants sets his sights on a beautiful Texas heiress. She clearly doesn't need his money, so *whatever* can she want with him? And when a police officer opens his door to a nine-months-pregnant stranger in the middle of a blizzard, he finds himself called on to provide both personal and professional services, in *Detective Daddy* by Jane Toombs.

So bundle up, and take heart—spring is coming! And so are six more sensational stories about love, life and family, coming next month from Silhouette Special Edition!

All the best,

Gail Chasan
Senior Editor

Please address questions and book requests to:
Silhouette Reader Service
U.S.: 3010 Walden Ave., P.O. Box 1325, Buffalo, NY 14269
Canadian: P.O. Box 609, Fort Erie, Ont. L2A 5X3

Books by Judy Duarte

Silhouette Special Edition

Cowboy Courage #1458
Family Practice #1511
Almost Perfect #1540
Big Sky Baby #1563
The Virgin's Makeover #1593
Bluegrass Baby #1598

Silhouette Books

Double Destiny
"Second Chance"

JUDY DUARTE,

an avid reader who enjoys a happy ending, always wanted to write books of her own. One day, she decided to make that dream come true. Five years and six manuscripts later, she sold her first book to Silhouette Special Edition.

Her unpublished stories have won the Emily and the Orange Rose awards, and in 2001 she became a double Golden Heart finalist. Judy credits her success to Romance Writers of America and two wonderful critique partners, Sheri WhiteFeather and Crystal Green, both of whom write for Silhouette.

At times, when a stubborn hero and a headstrong heroine claim her undivided attention, she and her family are thankful for fast food, pizza delivery and video games. When she's not at the keyboard or in a Walter Mitty–type world, she enjoys traveling, spending romantic evenings with her personal hero and playing board games with her kids.

Judy lives in Southern California and loves to hear from her readers. You may write to her at: P.O. Box 498, San Luis Rey, CA 92068-0498. You can also visit her Web site at: www.judyduarte.com.

Merlyn County Regional
Hospital Happenings

Congratulations to midwife Cecilia Mendoza on her engagement to our very own Bingham Enterprises executive Geoff Bingham! A combination bridal and baby shower for the happy couple is tentatively scheduled for late fall. Please see nurse Vanessa Harris for more details, or to volunteer for the decorating committee.

Detective Bryce Collins will be working alongside Dr. Mari Bingham on an investigation into procedures at the Foster Clinic. Please give the detective your full cooperation should he request information about the hospital. And please continue to report *any* strange behavior at the Foster Clinic or in the pharmacy department to Dr. Bingham or her receptionist.

Finally, a belated—but hearty—greeting to Dr. Kyle Bingham. Back in his hometown for a pediatrician residency, the handsome doctor has reformed his bad-boy ways in order to help the children of Merlyn County. Everyone—especially you single ladies—be sure to give him your warmest welcome!

Chapter One

Milla Johnson pressed the cell phone closer to her ear and glanced around the hospital cafeteria, glad no one could hear her conversation with her mother.

"The Binghams will turn on you," her mom said, "now that you've been named in that malpractice suit."

Milla rolled her eyes. She had enough stress in her life without her mother creating an enemy force out of the town's most prominent family.

"I worry about you," her mom added.

"I'm worried, too." Milla, a midwife for only a year, had been unfairly charged with malpractice, following the home birth of a baby girl. "That lawsuit could potentially end my career before it gets off the ground. And it could shut down the Foster Clinic's unique home-birth program.''

''That's what I mean about the Binghams turning on you.'' When Milla didn't respond, her mother asked, ''Did you hear what I said?''

Actually, the words rang loud and clear, but listening to unwelcome advice was another story. Especially when the Bingham family wasn't responsible for the lawsuit. ''I'm sorry, Mom. It's a bit noisy in here.''

Milla stared at the plate of meat loaf in front of her, then shoved it aside. She'd thought the mashed potatoes might sit well. Now she wasn't so sure. Her stomach had been a mess ever since learning of the malpractice suit, more so now that she'd talked to her mom.

''You watch your back, honey.''

''I'll be careful.'' Milla felt badly enough about being blamed for something that hadn't been her fault and for the problems the lawsuit would cause the Bingham Foundation. She didn't need a dose of maternal paranoia to complicate things.

Her mother had never made a secret of her distrust of the Binghams, but Milla was grateful to them. The family had done a lot for Merlyn County, and the Bingham Foundation had provided the grant that had paid for her midwifery education. True, she agreed to work for the clinic for the next five years to pay back the funds, but she loved her job and the professionals with whom she worked. She couldn't imagine working at another clinic. Or worse, if the plaintiffs had their way, not working as a midwife ever again.

"Those people have brought nothing but heartache to our family."

"By 'those people,'" you mean Billy Bingham in particular. And the man has been dead for eight years, Mom."

"Your aunt Connie died giving birth to one of Billy's illegitimate babies."

It was an age-old complaint and one Milla had grown tired of hearing. Her mother had never forgiven the man she blamed for her sister's death, a man who died in a plane crash months before his youngest son's birth.

Milla and her mother had raised the boy in their cramped, two-bedroom home since the day he was born. They both loved Dylan, in spite of his penchant for mischief. But oftentimes the money had been scarce, and even Milla had to admit life would have been easier on the Johnson household had Billy Bingham provided for Dylan the way he had for the other children he'd fathered without benefit of marriage.

Desperate to change the subject and to fast-forward the conversation she said, "I'm going to stop by the market on the way home. Do you need anything?"

"We're out of milk."

"Anything else?" While her mother recited a list, Milla glanced up and saw Dr. Kyle Bingham enter the busy cafeteria, and her heart skipped a beat.

The good-looking resident spotted her, too, and

grinned, sending a jolt of awareness to jump-start her pulse. Kyle had turned her head on more than one occasion, and the attraction seemed to be mutual.

He headed toward her table.

"Listen, Mom, I've got to go. I'll buy the groceries after I pick up Dylan from day camp. I'll talk to you later."

"Just remember what I said about the Binghams. Watch out."

"I will," Milla said, although the only thing she felt like watching was the blond Adonis coming her way. For some reason she didn't even want to ponder, his smile had the power to make her heart rate go absolutely bonkers.

Tall, broad-shouldered and more handsome than a man had a right to be, Kyle Bingham had a flashy wardrobe, a promising medical career and no financial worries, even after attending Harvard Medical School. The guy could have more than his share of women— and probably had. So the fact that he found Milla even remotely attractive was flattering. Thrilling.

As he approached her table, she tried to come up with a reason why she didn't need to get involved with him—anything other than her mother's warning.

"This chair taken?" Dr. Adonis asked.

"No." Milla shoved her phone back into her purse, setting it aside just as she had her mother's warning. Even if she'd wanted to be mindful of the well-intentioned maternal advice by avoiding the Bingham family—which Milla didn't—avoiding Kyle wasn't the same thing.

Kyle was one of Billy's illegitimate children. And from what Milla had heard, he didn't have much to do with the other Binghams who'd been blessed with legitimacy.

Of course, watching herself around the man for other reasons might be wise. The young pediatrician was a bit cocky and on the arrogant side, although Milla could understand why. Kyle Bingham was a brilliant young doctor, and he knew it. She couldn't fault him for having self-confidence.

Kyle took a seat across from her and cut right to the chase. "I want to testify on your behalf in that lawsuit."

"You do?" Relief washed over her, and she had to struggle not to fall at his feet and gush her appreciation. As the attending physician on call when Joe and Darlene Canfield had rushed their sick newborn to the E.R. of Merlyn County Regional Hospital, Kyle would make an excellent witness.

"You and I both know that umbilical infections don't happen at birth. That baby's illness wasn't caused by anything you did or failed to do."

Milla knew it hadn't been her fault. In spite of what the Canfields had said, she'd taken every precaution. She'd cut the cord textbook perfectly. And before she left the house, she'd told the new parents how to care for the umbilicus. She'd also advised them to bring the baby in for a postnatal exam, something they'd neglected to do.

"You have no idea how much I appreciate you saying that," she said.

"The Canfields had bandaged the umbilicus, which first alerted me to the probable cause of the infection."

Milla had told them to keep the umbilicus clean and dry. And she'd not only shown them how, she'd left them with printed instructions, although the lawsuit claimed she'd haphazardly cut the cord and left two new parents without any direction at all.

"After the baby stabilized, I took time to talk to Mrs. Canfield and question her. They hadn't cleaned the umbilicus properly, and in addition, the disposable diapers she was using were entirely too large, which irritated the stump. At that time, they applied the bandage."

"Which kept the umbilicus moist, instead of dry."

Kyle nodded. "Mrs. Canfield was also having nursing difficulties."

"Is she claiming that was my fault, too?" Milla asked. "I worked with her at length before leaving the house. The baby took right to the breast, and they didn't seem to be having any trouble."

"She didn't blame that on you. But I don't think she was comfortable breast-feeding, and I'm not sure how often she nursed the baby, which might have compromised the infant's immune system."

Milla blew out a sigh of relief, glad to have someone else realize she hadn't been at fault.

"The Canfields claim the umbilicus was already infected before they bandaged it," Kyle added, "which is probably the argument their attorney will use."

"So, even with your testimony, this lawsuit may not be settled easily."

"Who knows what will happen with the attorney involved. But the baby's infection wasn't your fault."

"And you'll testify to that?"

"Absolutely."

In her heart, she knew she'd done everything right during that delivery. But it was important to know that Kyle had agreed to testify for that reason alone, and not because he ultimately meant to protect the Binghams, the foundation and the clinic.

"And what if you thought the infection *had* been my fault?" Milla asked.

He leaned forward, assessed her as though she'd accused him of moral ineptitude. "I'd have no qualms about testifying against you or the Foster Clinic if I thought that infection had been caused by professional negligence."

For the first time since being served notice of the lawsuit, Milla began to breathe easier.

She had someone on her side.

And not just anyone.

Dr. Kyle Bingham.

"By the way," he said. "I've got to get back to

the E.R., but I wondered if you might like to have dinner with me tonight.''

Dinner? With the best-looking doctor in all of Merlyn County? Was it a professional meeting? Or was it more like a date? She couldn't be sure, yet when his blue gaze caught hers, her heart fluttered and something powerful passed between them.

Her mother would throw a walleyed fit—if she found out. But what Sharon Johnson didn't know wouldn't hurt her. Milla might live under her mom's roof, but not under her thumb. Their living arrangement had more to do with finances. And, more recently, Dylan's well-being.

"Sure," she told the handsome resident. "I'd like to have dinner with you."

"I'll pick you up around six, if you'll give me your address."

Uh-oh. That might not be a good idea. Milla wasn't up for another defensive bout with her mother this evening—not at this point in what might or might not develop into a relationship. She'd need time to work on her mom, more time than she would have between now and six o'clock. "Why don't I meet you at the restaurant?"

"All right, if you're more comfortable doing it that way." Kyle slid her a heart-stopping grin. "I'll see you at Melinda's. Around six."

Milla merely nodded, afraid her voice would betray her nervousness.

And her excitement.

* * *

At five minutes to six Milla pulled into Melinda's parking lot. The red brick building, once a firehouse, had been converted into a steak and seafood restaurant. Melinda's might not be as fancy as some restaurants found in Lexington, but it boasted an extensive wine list and was the fanciest eatery Merlyn County had to offer.

She parked her car, a white Caprice Classic whose odometer had lapped once or twice and still showed considerable mileage. But rather than opening the door, she continued to sit behind the wheel. Nervous. Apprehensive. And far more expectant than she cared to admit.

She spotted Kyle's black, late-model BMW parked close to the restaurant's entrance.

Waiting for her.

Milla Johnson.

Could she be any more flattered? She'd never had a man like Kyle interested in her.

Or had she read him wrong? Maybe he had only asked her here to discuss the lawsuit.

She'd wanted to primp before coming, to try on several outfits and fuss with her hair and makeup. But she'd feared her mother would notice and ask questions Milla didn't have time to answer, questions she'd have to skirt until she had time to set her mom straight about her personal life, about boundaries.

A quick glance in the mirror told Milla she looked

all right. Not bad. But deep inside she wanted to look her best.

As she climbed from the driver's seat and closed the car door, she heard a man's voice.

"Why, look there, Darlene. That's the woman who nearly killed our baby."

Milla's feet seemed to take root in the asphalt. She didn't need to see the man's face to know who it was. Joe Canfield, the father of the baby who'd been rushed into the E.R. burning with fever and its limp, little body racked with infection.

The baby girl she'd been accused of neglecting.

The baby Kyle Bingham had saved.

"Enjoy your night out on the town," Canfield said, as he and his wife strolled down the sidewalk that ran along Main Street. "When we get done with you, you'll be doing jail time."

Trying desperately to heed her attorney's advice and avoid any conversation—let alone a confrontation—with the plaintiffs, Milla strode toward the entrance of Melinda's. Her chest tightened to the point of making breathing difficult.

She clenched her fists, her nails biting into her palms. Tears of frustration welled in her eyes. Why were they doing this to her? The baby's infection hadn't been her fault.

All she wanted to do was hightail it home and lock the door behind her. For a moment, she'd considered getting back in her car and using her cell phone to call Kyle and postpone their dinner.

But maybe she needed to meet with him, to see him. To let him tell her all over again that the Canfield baby's life-threatening condition hadn't been her fault.

She needed the reassurance. She also needed the distraction. And an evening out with a doctor whose smile could turn her inside out would certainly help her forget her troubles, if only for tonight.

So instead of bolting, she held her head high and continued into the restaurant.

"Ms. Johnson?" the hostess asked.

Milla fingered the narrow shoulder strap of her black purse. "Yes."

"Dr. Bingham is waiting in the bar. If you'll follow me, I'll show you to his table."

Milla made her way across the polished concrete floor to the lounge, where a massive, carved-oak bar lined the back wall and a vast display of framed black-and-white photographs decorated the brick of the inside walls.

Kyle stood when she reached his table. He flashed her a dazzling smile that sent her tummy topsy-turvy and her heart soaring. She nearly forgot the unpleasant run-in she'd had with the Canfields.

Nearly, but not quite.

"Would you like something to drink?" he asked.

"White wine." *And plenty of it,* her nerves shouted in echoed concert.

Kyle motioned for the waitress, and before long

their drink order had been placed. "Our reservations are at six-thirty. I hope you don't mind waiting."

She managed a smile. "That's fine."

Trying to hide her nervousness, she turned to the brick wall and spotted the nearest photo. A small brass plaque said it was the first fire chief of Merlyn County dressed in a Santa Claus outfit and sitting at the wheel of a fire truck. She touched the wooden frame that had been bolted to the wall, then glanced at Kyle and caught him watching her.

He smiled. "I guess the proprietor wants to make sure tipsy, local history buffs can't run off with any of the old photos."

Before Milla could respond, the waitress brought a Merlot for him and a Chardonnay for her.

Kyle lifted his wineglass in a toast. "To the start of a friendship."

A friendship? For the briefest moment, Milla wrestled with disappointment. A part of her, a very young and romantic side she'd almost forgotten about, had hoped for more.

But when her gaze snagged his and she spotted the vibrant sparkle in those baby blues, she realized he had more than friendship on his mind. And so did she. But with her inexperience, at least with guys like Kyle, she wasn't sure how far she wanted things to go. Still, the idea of letting this night play out romantically intrigued her and sent a warm sense of anticipation coursing through her blood.

She took a sip of wine, then studied him over the

rim. He was gorgeous. And charming. And no doubt, a bit of a playboy, the way his dad had been.

Was Kyle Bingham the kind of man she should avoid?

Or the kind of man every woman needed to experience at least once in her life?

Unwilling to give in to either wonder or indecision, she eyed him carefully, as though she knew exactly what they both wanted. Her hormones seemed to kick up a notch. And sexual curiosity appeared to be on the rampage.

What would it be like to touch him, to kiss him, to lose herself in the passion that blazed in his eyes?

She looked at him, as though he might explain the attraction that crackled between them like an electrical storm. But he just sat there, waiting.

Watching her.

Kyle found himself practically gawking at the young midwife who'd caught his eye on more than one occasion since he'd arrived in Merlyn County a few months ago.

Damn. Milla Johnson was one beautiful woman, although she didn't seem to be aware of it. She'd dressed simply in a classic black dress. And she hadn't done much to her chestnut-colored hair, other than brush it until it shined. The ends seemed to naturally curl under in a sophisticated style.

She was the kind of woman who stood out in a

crowd. The kind of woman who made his libido sit up and beg.

He usually complimented the lady he was with as a means of breaking the ice and gaining an advantage. But tonight, the words came easy. "You look pretty, Milla."

She flushed at his comment, then smiled, flashing him two dimples he could get used to seeing. "Thank you."

The women Kyle usually dated were fully aware of their beauty, their sexuality. Milla, although just as lovely and attractive, wasn't as sure of herself, which, for some reason, pleased him, making her all the more appealing.

She took a sip of wine, then ran her tongue across her bottom lip.

A surge of heat shot through Kyle's bloodstream, arousing him, tempting him. She glanced again at the photos on the wall, completely oblivious, it seemed, of the effect she was having on him.

Kyle leaned back in his chair, unbalanced by his arousal and by the effect she had on him. The pretty midwife had stirred a powerful hunger, one that dinner at Melinda's wouldn't sate.

It was early yet, and there was no reason for him to believe the evening would end with anything more than a handshake. Which would be a shame. He couldn't remember being this attracted to a woman in a long time.

She set her wineglass on the linen-covered table

and looked at him. Her big brown eyes bore evidence of a trying day.

"What's the matter?"

She fingered the cocktail napkin that rested under her wineglass, rolling the edge then unrolling it. "I almost didn't come inside."

"Are you sorry you're here?" He hoped not. Milla had stirred something inside of him. And not just sexual attraction. There were other things going on, too. Admiration. Respect. Milla Johnson was a dedicated professional who had a genuine concern for her patients. And she had a depth to her that the other women he dated didn't have.

"I ran into Joe Canfield outside." Her voice softened, and she looked at him with Bambi eyes that made him want to tear into the guy who'd upset her.

"He wasn't very nice," she added.

Kyle reached across the table, taking Milla's hand—a move that probably surprised them both. But he quickly recovered. "Don't let that guy get to you. You didn't do anything wrong, and the judge ought to be able to see through him."

She nodded, but her vulnerability smacked him upside the heart, making him wish he could protect her from all the things that went bump in the night. His soft side didn't surface very often, yet it struck with a vengeance tonight.

Before they finished their drinks, the hostess led them to a quiet booth in the dining room and handed them menus.

The waiter brought a basket of warm bread and placed it on the table. Kyle welcomed the interruption. And as he reached for the golden-brown loaf, Milla did the same. Their hands brushed, shocking him with a tingle of heat that lasted long after the brief contact. Neither of them commented, yet her silent gaze told Kyle she'd felt it, too.

They remained pensive for a while, engrossed in the entrées Melinda's offered, Kyle supposed, although he was far more interested in getting through dinner and seeing what pleasures the rest of the evening might bring.

Milla set her menu to the side of her place setting and leaned slightly forward. "What made you decide to be a doctor?"

Her question took him aback, since most people asked why he'd chosen pediatrics, a specialty that surprised anyone who'd known him growing up.

Kyle had always been prone to mischief, a result of being one of Billy Bingham's brats, he supposed. As a kid, he'd gotten a reputation for snaking his way out of trouble. But there didn't seem to be any use going into that.

"When I was fifteen, a couple of buddies and I went on an overnight campout at a lake near the house where I grew up. We barbecued hamburgers for dinner." Kyle studied the flickering candle that sat in the middle of the linen-draped table. He didn't like to talk about that day, maybe because the memory still clawed at his chest and throat.

Milla leaned forward, listening. Casting some kind of healing balm on the pain he'd harbored and the utter helplessness he'd felt as he watched a strong, robust kid dwindle away, plagued by an unknown disease.

"My best friend, Jimmy Hoben, liked his meat rare," Kyle continued.

She didn't respond, but her eyes shared her compassion, her sympathy, her understanding.

"A few days later, Jimmy got sick. Really sick. And the doctors had a hell of a time figuring out what was wrong with him. Even after they realized his illness was caused by e-coli, the damage had been done. And in spite of everything they did, every medication and treatment they tried, Jimmy didn't make it."

"I'm sorry," she said.

"It was a tough thing for everyone, I guess. Especially a kid like me." His voice bore the huskiness of emotion he'd tried to bury years ago. "I couldn't figure out why modern medicine couldn't heal my friend. Or others like him. In fact, I was so determined to get some answers, that I went to the library and hit the books, trying to learn everything I could about e-coli and the effect it had on the human body. That focus triggered a deep interest in medicine. And research."

She nodded in understanding, but maybe that's because she hadn't known him growing up. Hadn't known the hell-raiser he'd once been.

When he told his high school guidance counselor

that he'd decided to go to medical school, the guy had been shocked. But in spite of the counselor's disbelief, Kyle made a dramatic academic turnaround, which surprised the entire teaching staff, as well as all of his friends. Within one semester, his teachers and peers were amazed when the campus bad boy aced every class.

"I found my niche in human biology and anatomy," he said.

"So you decided to be a doctor."

"Sort of." He shrugged, then slid her a crooked grin. "Actually, when my residency is done, I'm going into research."

"Around here?" she asked.

"No. Back in Boston. I have no intention of staying in Merlyn County longer than the time it takes me to complete my residency." He could have explained that his decision to stay here that long was a way of compromising with his mother, of making her happy until he moved on for good.

His playboy daddy had provided well for his illegitimate kids, particularly Kyle. And for that reason, Kyle had been able to attend Harvard medical school. His mom hoped that he would eventually make his home in Merlyn County and take up his rightful place with the Binghams.

But Kyle had no intention of elbowing into his father's family.

"That's too bad," Milla said. "You're a great pediatrician and have a lot to offer the community."

He shrugged. "Maybe so. But I can do more good at a research hospital."

"To study pediatric pathology?"

"Kids shouldn't die before they get a chance to live." Kyle didn't usually open up like this, but for some reason it felt right sharing memories and dreams with Milla. Dinner was over before he knew it.

As the waiter took the last of their plates away, Kyle studied the woman across from him. The candlelight glistened off the strands of her hair, bathing her in a romantic glow. Tonight, more than ever, she had some kind of blood-pumping effect on him.

She declined coffee and dessert, which was fine with him. But he wasn't ready for the evening to end, not even after he'd paid the bill and walked her out to where she'd parked her car.

His hands ached to reach out and pull her near. But he waited, biding his time until Milla gave him reason to believe she would welcome his touch. He wasn't sure why, but this particular woman made him feel like an awkward adolescent with a bad haircut and a ketchup stain on his white T-shirt. And he hadn't felt that way since he'd had sex for the first time. After that, his confidence level had skyrocketed.

Until this moment.

The summer night was silent, save for the sound of their shoes crunching on the pavement. And the parking lot, now nearly empty, reminded Kyle it was time to call it a day. To end the pleasant evening they'd shared.

Milla paused by the car door, and her eyes caught his. Something passed between them; although, for the life of him, he wasn't sure what it was. If it hadn't rocked his sex drive to the core, he might have been scared and looked for a reason to escape. As it was, he stood still, savoring the woman and the moment.

A full moon peered from a lone cloud in the evening sky, watching over them, it seemed.

Always relaxed and confident with women, Kyle wasn't sure what had gotten into him. Maybe it was the moonlight dancing in a star-filled summer sky. And maybe it was the fact he hadn't had sex since coming back to Merlyn County. Or maybe it was some kind of spell Milla Johnson had cast on him.

Either way, he couldn't imagine letting her drive away without brushing his lips across hers. And as he did so, she wrapped her arms around him, pulling him close, allowing the kiss to deepen and their tongues to touch and taste.

She whimpered softly, and he was lost in a swirl of heat, a fire of desire.

A sense of urgency swept over him, and he pulled her close, felt her fingers snake through his hair. A jolt of heat damn near sent him over the edge, and he wanted more. Far more than he could have, standing out in the open, in a parking lot.

He wanted this woman. Tonight.

The strength of his desire should have scared him, should have caused him to turn tail and get his happy-to-be-a-bachelor butt out of Dodge.

Instead he savored her scent, her touch, and lost himself in one of the most arousing kisses he'd ever had.

Still, it didn't take him long to realize this public display of raw, sexual hunger needed to be taken indoors. With great reluctance he broke the kiss long enough to whisper against the silky strands of her hair.

"Come home with me."

Chapter Two

Come home with me.

As the words echoed through Milla's core, her own physical need chimed in.

Kyle wanted her. And she wanted him, too. The strength of her arousal surprised her, as did the decision hovering in the sultry night air.

Her knees still wobbly from the sensual assault of Kyle's mouth, she tried to catch her breath, to gain control of her runaway desire. But she wasn't having any luck.

Kyle leaned against the side of her car. Had his knees nearly given out on him, too?

Their bodies no longer touched, but his gaze held her transfixed. "There's something powerful going on between us."

He had that right. The kiss they'd shared had been so hot, so unlike anything she'd ever experienced, that her ability to think or reason seemed to have disappeared. For good.

And right now she wasn't so sure that was a bad thing. Her feelings were too strong, charged and close to the surface.

"You feel it, too," he told her.

She nodded. "Yes, I do."

"What are we going to do about it?"

As she saw it, they had two options. She could get in her car and drive away, knowing regret would follow her home. And this darn whatever-it-was would haunt her every time their paths crossed.

Or a second and more pleasing option—she could throw caution to the wind. Do something wild for a change. Experience something she might never experience again.

She could make love to Kyle Bingham, resident heartthrob of Merlyn County Regional Hospital. If his kiss could turn her inside out, what would their lovemaking be like?

They hadn't closed the sexually charged gap between them, yet she could hear his heart pounding, feel his blood rushing through his veins. Or was that her own?

"Let's take this inside," he said. "Behind closed doors."

Milla knew she should pull herself together and

graciously decline. But the fact of the matter was she wanted more of Kyle's kisses, more of his touch.

And she wanted it now.

He stepped toward her and brushed a strand of hair from her cheek. His heated gaze drew her into the sexual depths of something she couldn't resist.

"All right." Her voice held a seductive edge she'd never noticed before. And when the words left her mouth, she didn't regret them. Not at all.

He caught her cheek in his hand and brought his mouth to hers in a hot, breath-stealing kiss that spoke a promise—not of forever, but of fulfillment.

But that's all she needed tonight.

Fulfillment.

To feel competent and capable, no longer shaken by the unfairness of the Canfields' charges. To have her confidence restored in the arms of a doctor who made her heart soar and her blood race.

"Okay. Let's go," she said. "You lead the way."

They each climbed into their cars, and she followed Kyle to the outskirts of town, where he turned down a quiet little street called Bluebonnet Lane. His black BMW pulled under a carport near the end unit of a sage-colored triplex flanked by duplexes on each side. She parked on the street.

Funny, she'd imagined him living somewhere else, someplace expensive and grand. Not that it mattered, of course.

He opened her door in a gentlemanly manner, then helped her from the car.

"I bought these units as an investment," Kyle said, as he led her to the front door. "My mom lives in one side of the first duplex. She's a proud lady and won't let me help her out financially. So we reached a compromise. She watches out for the other units in exchange for rent. When I move back to Boston, she'll oversee this one, too."

When he let her inside the small home, she wasn't sure what to expect. Something to match his *GQ* clothing and his flashy car, she supposed. Instead she found the living room had been decorated simply. A plain brown sofa. White walls. Miniblinds on the window overlooking the street. His place was clean and almost sterile.

The only thing that stood out was a big-screen television that seemed out of place.

"I'm not home often," he said, as though reading her thoughts. "I couldn't see any point in buying furniture or in putting anything on the walls. I've got all I need."

She nodded, scanning the sparse, uncluttered room, unable to keep from wondering if he ever felt lonely in a place that seemed to be little more than four walls, a sofa and a theater-size TV.

"Can I get you something to drink?" he asked, his voice low, almost quiet. "A glass of wine, maybe?"

The attraction between them remained hot, yet neither moved.

Was Kyle nervous, too? The dapper doctor who had every single midwife and nurse on staff at the clinic and the hospital giggling and whispering like girls with a crush on the new boy at school?

Maybe so.

The thought pleased her and made her feel feminine and powerful. The arousing effect only bolstered her confidence in the decision she'd made to follow him home.

She tucked a strand of hair behind her ear and smiled. "I don't think either of us came here wanting more to drink."

He tossed her a crooked grin, and all signs of nervousness fell away. "You're right. I was just trying to be a good host."

Feeling bolder than she'd ever felt before, Milla stepped closer, reached a hand to his cheek, brushed a thumb across his angular jaw and felt the tingle from the faint bristle of his beard. "Maybe one more kiss will make this easier for both of us."

She'd barely lifted her lips to his when he took the lead, took her tongue and took her breath away.

Lordy, how that man could kiss.

Milla lost herself in the wet, velvety confines of Kyle's mouth. And in the heat of his embrace, reality slipped away and magic took its place, releasing a display of mystical fireworks that lit her heart and soul.

Kyle wasn't sure what it was about Milla that swept him away, but he wasn't about to analyze it, not when he held her in his arms and felt her breasts splayed against his chest as she leaned into his demanding erection.

He'd never lost himself in a woman before, hadn't ever expected to, but he seemed to be momentarily losing himself in Milla, in her kiss and the soft swirl of her springtime scent. He might be sorry later, but that's when he would think about it.

Later. After he'd buried himself in her softness, lost himself in the passion that plagued them both. There was a heat in Milla's touch, a fire in her kiss. And he couldn't seem to get enough of her.

She tugged at his shirt, pulling it from the waistband of his slacks, and then grabbed at his belt, freeing him. Freeing them both.

All the while, her mouth held his in sweet surrender. Her fingers blazed a trail along his skin, singeing his nerve endings.

He reached for the zipper of her dress, unleashing the black cotton, and he slipped the garment off her shoulders. He wanted to feel her skin on his, breasts to chest. And he doubted they could remove their clothes fast enough.

But Kyle wasn't about to take Milla on the living room floor, not this time, anyway. With reluctance, he broke the kiss and took her hand. "Come with me." Then he led her down the hall and into the bedroom.

She stood before him by the king-size bed. Her dress had fallen to the waist, revealing a satiny black bra over hardened and responsive nipples. A sexual flush blazed across her throat and chest, announcing a desire every bit as strong as his.

He cupped her face, brushed a thumb across the silky texture of her cheek and saw the glaze of passion in those pretty brown eyes. "You're a beautiful woman, Milla."

She blushed, and again he was taken by her lack of pretense. Couldn't she see what he saw?

"I want to make this special for you." And damn it, he did. There was something virginal about her, something sweet and innocent. But she didn't kiss him like a virgin or touch him like one.

She pushed her dress over her hips, then stepped out of the garment and stood before him in skimpy black undergarments. He watched as she unhooked her bra and freed two perfect breasts. His breath caught, and his testosterone raged.

What was it about this woman that made her seem so different from the others?

"Make love to me, Kyle." Then she unbuttoned his shirt and pressed herself to him, stoking a blaze deep within him.

He tore himself from her embrace, just long enough to dig through the nightstand drawer for a condom. His efforts were thwarted by haste and desire, as he fumbled with the foil packet and tried to protect them both.

When he joined her on the bed, their hungry kiss resumed and tongues mated in a lover's frenzy. Caught up in a fire that might never burn out, Kyle realized his only hope for relief was to bury himself in her.

As he entered, she arched up to meet him, and he was lost. Lost in lust and passion.

Kyle had wanted their first time together to be special, but all he could think about was how good it felt to be inside of her, to have her meet each of his thrusts, to be shaken to the core by a powerful climax that made her cry out in pleasure and damn near turned him inside out.

He'd wanted to love her with a slow hand, taking the time to make tonight memorable for them both, since a continuing relationship wasn't wise and certainly wasn't in his game plan. But his fiery passion burned out of control.

When he'd had a chance to catch his breath and grow hard again, he would take it slow and easy, making sure the rest of the night was every bit as good as it could be.

But for the time being, he would hold her until the last wave of pleasure ebbed.

Milla glanced at the clock on the wall—3:00 a.m. The scent of lovemaking filled the air, and her naked body still hummed from the last sweet joining, just an hour before.

Kyle held her close, one of his arms tucked under her waist and the other draped across her breasts. His gentle breathing told her he was asleep, contented and sated.

But she wasn't.

Well, she was definitely sated. Their lovemaking had been great—mindless and hot, but fulfilling.

She'd found much-needed comfort, as well as pleasure, in Kyle's arms. But after the loving, when her conscience had a chance to sneak in and shake a finger at her, contentment slipped by the wayside.

Making love to Kyle had seemed right, but in the wee hours of the morning, after the waves of the last powerful climax had ceased, her good sense returned.

Her conscience, which had deserted her earlier in the evening, surfaced with a vengeance. Yes, she'd willingly followed Kyle home. And she'd enjoyed the best lovemaking she'd ever known. Not that she had anything to compare it to—one boyfriend in college who'd been a mistake from the get go.

She'd wanted to make love to Kyle, and he hadn't disappointed her. He was a great lover, considerate and gifted in the fine art of seduction and pleasure. Of course, that was probably because he'd had so much practice.

But Milla hadn't been thinking clearly. Her head had been in a romantic cloud and her hormones had taken over.

While in Melinda's parking lot, making out like a couple of teenagers, she hadn't given a hoot about what her mother might say. But now, after the loving, she realized her mother would never understand Milla having a relationship of any kind with Kyle.

Not that Milla hadn't crossed her mom on other

occasions and weathered the storm. Truthfully, Milla dating a Bingham would be a big thorn in her mother's backside, but their mother-daughter relationship wouldn't suffer any serious consequences.

More troublesome than her mother's disapproval was that Milla had become intimately involved with a co-worker. What if word of their...indiscretion leaked out?

That problem, she supposed, could also be dealt with.

But the next accusation her conscience hurled at her struck hard, knocking the wind out of her like a tumble from a tree and a belly flop on the lawn.

What if the Canfields learned that Milla and the pediatrician who would testify in her defense were sleeping together?

Things were certain to get uglier than they already were.

Sure, Milla and Kyle both knew the Canfields didn't have a case. But malpractice suits didn't have to be based on medical logic. The Canfields could sue—and win—without having any concrete medical evidence. If taken to court, the publicity alone would hurt the Janice Foster Clinic, as well as Milla's reputation. And the case would also result in higher malpractice insurance premiums for her and the clinic.

No, the problems the malpractice suit could bring hadn't disappeared. And, in fact, they had probably been compounded by her decision to make love to the doctor who would testify on her behalf.

Kyle slept soundly, obviously having no qualms about their night of passion.

But Milla had plenty of reservations. And regrets. No matter how good it had been.

Carefully slipping away from his embrace, she quietly dressed and tiptoed from his room. She grabbed her purse and heels from the living room, not taking time to slip on her shoes, and stole out of the house.

A small, adolescent voice inside called out, *Hey! What about Kyle? What about what we just shared?*

But Milla needed to face the truth. There couldn't be anything between her and Kyle. Not now.

What if he calls? the young voice cried. *What will you tell him?*

The voice of reason stepped in to answer. *Kyle is probably a player, just like his dad—a guy who loved whatever lady he was with.*

If Kyle called her—which wasn't likely, given his playboy daddy's blood—she'd tell him their…intimacy had been a mistake.

Milla Johnson had enough to worry about without the complications a relationship with Kyle Bingham would bring.

Chapter Three

Milla arrived home while the stars still glittered in the morning sky.

Once inside the small, darkened bedroom she shared with her mother, she moved quietly, but only as a courtesy—not out of fear of discovery. Milla had never had any trouble standing up to her mom when they'd had confrontations. But she was much too tired to stir things up now.

"Is that you, honey?" her mom asked, voice heavy with sleep.

"Yes, it's me. I'm sorry for waking you."

"It's all right. Those babies never choose a convenient time to be born, do they?"

Milla bit her lip and held back a response. As a

midwife, she'd spent many nights at the bedside of a laboring woman, providing obstetrical skill and support. It was a job she loved, a career in which she thrived despite its demands on her time.

It was natural for Sharon Johnson to assume her daughter had been working.

Milla had always been honest, even if that honesty ruffled a few maternal feathers, but she couldn't bring herself to speak or to respond one way or the other.

She looked at her mother's blanketed form and watched as her mom tugged at the covers, rolled over, faced the wall and blocked out the nocturnal intrusion, intending to go back to sleep. The woman was completely and blissfully unaware that her daughter had spent most of the night locked in Kyle Bingham's arms.

Milla hadn't lied—exactly. Of course, God probably kept a count of those pesky omissions, but she was too tired to think about that now. Too tired to feel guilty.

Well, too tired to feel guilty about anything other than making love to a man her mother wouldn't approve of. An experienced lover who'd taken her to the heights of sexual pleasure, again and again, coaxing multiple orgasms with ease.

Milla blew out a weary sigh and drew back the comforter that covered her twin bed. Then she climbed between the freshly laundered sheets, hoping to get an hour or two of sleep before dawn. But it was a hope that didn't stand a snowball's chance in hell.

An overactive mind kept her awake, taunting her with heated memories of a passion-filled night in the competent hands of an Adonis, a man she never should have kissed, let alone…

Had she clawed his back? Cried out in orgasmic release?

Yes, she had.

Kyle had brought out something wild and wicked in a usually levelheaded Milla. It both pleased and disturbed her.

At sunrise Milla gave up the struggle for rest. She showered, then started her workday sleep deprived—something she never did.

Even when she'd stayed up all night with a woman in labor, there was a sweet rush that came with delivering a baby into loving arms. A pleasant release of adrenaline that kept Milla going, awake and alert, ready to start the day.

But this was different. There was no adrenaline rush, no sense of self-satisfaction.

And Milla wasn't at all ready to face Kyle again.

Going through the motions at work, Milla wondered whether her shift at the clinic would ever end. All she wanted to do was go home, climb back into bed and crash.

Just before noon, while Milla checked her list of afternoon appointments, Crystal Hendrix, a nurse at the clinic, handed her a note. "Dr. Bingham called while you were with Mrs. Thompson. He's in the E.R. at the hospital and would like you to give him a call."

"Thanks." Milla hoped Crystal hadn't noticed her hands shake when she took the note. She glanced at it briefly, then shoved the paper into the pocket of her white coat.

Milla wasn't ready to speak to Kyle. What was she supposed to say? "Thanks for the great sex?"

Most women would be dying for another date, a repeat performance. But not Milla. And her reasons were legion, as were the vast array of emotions she'd grown tired of contemplating.

Maybe she'd just state the simple truth.

Dr. Kyle Bingham and Milla Johnson shouldn't have become involved. For professional reasons.

Yes, that's what she would tell him. When she returned his call, of course.

But that wouldn't happen today. Not when her mind was rheumy and her body tired.

Milla glanced at her wristwatch, then back at her list of patients. Maybe she could cut out early today, after seeing Sue Ellen Henderson at three o'clock. Then she could zip over to the school, pick up Dylan and head home.

She would call Kyle tomorrow.

Or maybe the day after that.

Milla pulled her car into the parking lot at Daniel Boone Elementary, where the school district sponsored a summer program for kids. The gray brick building with dirty white trim sat before her like a ghost town. It was summer and the kids were all out on the playground or in one of the four white trailers that served as temporary classrooms. She wondered if the school district planned to paint and repair the building before fall.

She hoped so. A bright and clean learning environment would benefit all the kids, not just Dylan, who struggled academically. Her eight-year-old cousin was bright and sweet, but for some reason he couldn't seem to stay focused and on track. Neither could he stay out of trouble.

Milla had asked his pediatrician about an organic cause to Dylan's behavior and had been assured there wasn't one.

Dylan was as cute and sweet as a kid could be, with blond hair, an unruly cowlick, big blue eyes and a splatter of freckles across his nose. And he was affectionate, too. But he just seemed to gravitate toward mischief.

Since the car accident that left her mother with chronic back and neck pain three years ago, most of Dylan's care had landed on Milla's shoulders, but she didn't mind. She'd fallen in love with that little boy when he was just a scrawny, seven-pound, red-faced infant who'd been placed in her arms. And from that day on, the two of them had developed a closeness, a special bond. But even Milla couldn't seem to help Dylan stay out of trouble.

As she reached the playground, she spotted Mr. Rick at the sign-out table, talking to a little boy Milla didn't recognize. She'd always thought Rick was the man's first name and the mister was a way of affording him more respect. But just the other day, she'd learned that Rick was a shortened form of Rickentaffer or Rickelstoffer or something like that.

As she approached the table, the tall, gangly man stood, and the serious look on his face spoke volumes. He didn't have to tell her that there'd been trouble again today.

"Dylan is in the rest room," Mr. Rick said. "He's got a bloody nose, and Mr. Gordon is cleaning him."

"What happened?"

"He and another boy were fighting behind the handball courts. They've been given a time out. If that doesn't work, we're going to ask them both to stay home for a few days." Mr. Rick took a deep breath and sighed. "Dylan's not a bad kid."

Milla knew that. But trouble seemed to follow him like a swirling, funnel-shaped cloud of dust. And when it caught up with him, Dylan couldn't seem to stay out of the way.

"He fought with Kirk Brower," the young man added, as though that explained it all.

Several times this summer, Kirk, a heavyset, red-headed kid with a reputation for being a bully, had taunted Dylan about being one of Billy's brats.

Like Dylan, the other third-grader hadn't known Billy Bingham and couldn't possibly have been aware of the man's reputation. The only logical explanation was that he'd overheard an adult comment. And Milla found that idea irritating. If she knew who to confront or how to quiet the gossip, she would have taken action. As it was, she could only hope that the whole thing would die a quick and easy death and that Dylan could ignore the comments until it did.

"Here he comes now," Mr. Rick said, nodding toward the rest room.

The two boys, Dylan and Kirk, came out of the bathroom with Mr. Gordon. When Dylan spotted her, he dropped his eyes and kicked the toe of his worn tennis shoe at the dirt, then continued to trudge toward her, head hung as though making his way down the long green mile.

Dylan's cheeks were red from exertion—or maybe remorse. His face, still damp from being bathed with a paper towel, bore dirt streaks near the hairline and over his brow. Blood splatters stained a torn white T-shirt. When he looked up at her, his blue eyes grew watery, but he blinked rapidly, as though trying to keep his feelings a secret.

Milla glanced at Kirk, who wore a smirk on his pudgy face. Like a big sister, she wanted to throttle the bully herself, but she took on the role of parent instead. "We'll talk about this in the car, Dylan."

Then she led the boy away, wishing she'd arrived sooner, before the scuffle that had bloodied his nose, before the cruel words had been spoken.

She doubted Dylan was the only one of Billy Bingham's illegitimate children to suffer taunts growing up, but it hurt her to see her young cousin teased for something that wasn't his fault. She ran a hand along the blond strands of his hair, felt the dirt and sand he'd accumulated during the day, probably during the fight.

"I'm sorry for getting in trouble again," he said. "But Kirk the Jerk is the stupidest kid in the whole school. In the whole world."

To say the least, Milla thought. "I hate to tell you this, but the world is full of Kirk the Jerks. And you can't fight them all. You're going to have to learn to hold your temper and ignore the cruel words."

The childhood ditty came to mind. *Sticks and stones may break my bones, but words will never hurt me.*

She didn't mention it to Dylan. Because she knew it wasn't true. Some words could do a lot of damage to a small boy's self-esteem.

"I know it hurts when kids tease," she added.

"He said I was a nobody. That I didn't have a real family because I don't have a mom or a dad." The boy's pain hung in the air, belying the next words he spoke. "But who needs a mom or a dad?"

A kid needed both. Milla knew that from her own experience. She'd only been ten when her dad left. She could still hear the slamming of the screen door. Could still remember running after him, hanging on to the door handle of his pickup truck, begging him to stay. "Daddy, wait!"

"I can't take it anymore," he'd told her, before pushing her aside. Then he'd rolled up the window and revved the engine. And when she stood back, he'd driven down the graveled drive. Out of town. Out of her life forever.

She'd never learned what it was that he couldn't take. Marriage to her mom? Responsibility? Milla had asked her mother, but the woman had refused to discuss it.

As a child, Milla had wondered what she'd done wrong, what she could have done to make her daddy stay. As a grown-up, she knew better than to blame herself for a choice her father had made. But every now and then, if she allowed herself to dwell on it, she still felt the pain of abandonment.

She slipped an arm around the boy, her heart going out to him. Even though neither Aunt Connie nor Billy had abandoned Dylan on purpose, the child was left without either parent.

Sure he had a loving guardian, but her mother's chronic back and neck pain didn't allow her to play catch or take him camping.

"I know I'm just your cousin," Milla said. "But if you want me to be your mom, it's okay with me."

"It is?" he asked, glancing at her with seeking eyes and a quivering lip.

"Sure." Milla stopped walking and turned to face the boy, cupping his cheeks with her hands. She kissed his sweaty, dirt-streaked brow, then pulled him close, savoring the kid-size strength of his hug. "I've always wanted a son like you."

"You have?" he asked, voice incredulous. "I'd like you to be my mom, Milla. That would be way cool."

A tear dripped down her cheek, but she didn't see the need to brush it away or hide it.

There wasn't much she could do to change the reality Dylan lived with each day. But in her own way she could make a difference. She could take a more active parental-type role with him, create the kind of family she'd never had but always wanted.

The kind of family Dylan needed.

Minus a dad, of course.

A concise excerpt of the words Dylan had spoken only moments before came to mind.

Who needed a dad?

Not Milla. And not Dylan. Men like their fathers were often more trouble than they were worth.

She'd be selective when it came time to choose a husband. For some reason a certain blond doctor came to mind. A man whose smile warmed her soul, whose touch heated her blood. They'd had something special that night, something fulfilling.

But Milla quickly shoved the sexual memory aside. Wants and needs were two different things. She might want to spend another night in Kyle Bingham's arms, but she needed to have a working relationship with him. And she needed him to testify on her behalf.

Yet a little voice spoke in the stillness, reminding

her there was one more reason to stay away from a man like Kyle, a very important reason.

Milla didn't need anyone with the power to turn her life on end.

Or to walk away when he grew tired of her.

Chapter Four

Kyle wasn't sure what had gone wrong between him and Milla, but he sure as hell didn't need to chase after her. Not when he wasn't after any kind of commitment from her. Or from anyone, for that matter. He enjoyed being free to come and go as he pleased, to date whomever he wanted.

But Milla had left his bed without saying goodbye, without asking for anything—whether he was willing to give it or not.

And that bothered him more than he cared to admit.

He'd called her at the clinic the next morning, while she'd been with a patient, but she hadn't returned his call. He supposed there was always the possibility that Crystal, the nurse who'd taken the message, had neglected to tell Milla.

The idea that his one-time lover might be avoiding him left him a bit bewildered, if truth be told. Women had a tendency to cling to Kyle, to make him set boundaries in a relationship.

They didn't ignore his calls.

As he stepped outside the hospital for some much-needed fresh air, he spotted Milla outside the Foster Clinic, sitting under a tree and eating a sack lunch. She hadn't seen him yet. And she seemed lost in her own thoughts. Maybe now was a good time to talk to her.

He cut across the lawn, felt the sunlight on his face, caught the sound of a lark in one of the trees overhead. As he approached, she glanced up.

Had her eyes widened in surprise?

"Hey," he said by way of greeting. "You look comfortable."

She didn't, though. She looked more like a skittish fawn caught in the meadow alone. She offered him a shy smile that looked forced. Brittle. "Hi."

Okay, so his instincts had been right. She'd been avoiding him. For some reason, that didn't sit well.

"Let's talk about the other night." The words flowed from Kyle's mouth without any effort on his part, surprising him. He usually wasn't one to bring up intimate subjects.

But he didn't like the idea of Milla going her own separate way without talking to him. He didn't like it at all. Even in his love-'em-and-leave-'em days he had shown more courtesy than that.

She set her sandwich on the napkin covering her lap. "You're right. We should talk about it."

"Are you having regrets?" He wasn't sure why he asked, since regret was written all over her pretty face.

"We shouldn't have become involved like that, under the circumstances." She bit her bottom lip, then looked at him as though he should know exactly what was on her mind.

"What circumstances are those?"

She paused for a while, trying hard to be tactful, or so it seemed. "I don't think it's a good idea for us to date, since we work together."

She was implying professional ethics played a part in her rejection, but he figured there was more to it than that. She'd known the circumstances before this…this affair or whatever it was. She'd known it when they'd had dinner, while they'd made out like teenagers in the parking lot. And she'd known it after following him home.

If it hadn't bothered her then, why now?

Because of your father, you idiot.

Where had that archaic insecurity come from? Kyle had put that bastard stigma out of his mind years ago, ever since going off to college.

But he'd moved back to Merlyn County. And for some damn reason, the memory of the scorn he'd grown up with rushed to the forefront of his mind today, reminding him of who he was and where he'd come from.

His mom had been ostracized from her community, a small town outside of Binghamton, after falling for Billy Bingham's charms and bearing his firstborn son without the benefit of marriage.

As a kid, Kyle had felt as if no one truly accepted him, including his father and the entire legitimate branch of the Bingham family. It had seemed as if they were all waiting for him to screw up.

He'd since come to grips with his illegitimacy, but Milla's comment ruffled the shame he'd tried hard to bury. "Does this have anything to do with my father?"

"No," she told him, yet she worried her lip, suggesting she might be lying or holding something back. Suggesting that her predawn disappearance did have something to do with his paternity.

"But?" he prodded her to continue, to admit what was really bothering her. And he almost hated himself for doing it.

What did he care? Milla Johnson wasn't the only pretty young woman in Merlyn County.

Yet, right now, she was the only one who interested him.

She blew out a sigh. "I'm not sure whether you know this or not, and it certainly doesn't make a difference to me, but my aunt Connie died giving birth to one of your father's kids."

Kyle's footloose daddy had sure gotten around. A carefree bachelor who spent money like water and captured the heart of almost every girl in the county, the late Billy Bingham had fathered a passel of kids, all of whom he'd taken care of. Three carried the Bingham family name, while several others preferred not to be acknowledged.

Growing up as one of Billy's brats, Kyle could certainly understand why. In fact, he'd often thought his own life would have been a hell of a lot more tolerable had his mother chosen not to give Kyle his father's name.

Milla's cousin was one of the siblings Kyle hadn't known about.

"So, sleeping with your cousin's half brother makes you uneasy. Or is it more than that?"

"No, I'm okay with it." Milla wrapped the remains of her sandwich in the napkin and dropped it into the paper bag resting on the lawn beside her. She stood and met his gaze. "My mom still harbors a lot of resentment toward your father. But I don't. The reason we shouldn't see each other is because we work together. A relationship would make things…sticky."

He supposed she had a point, but regret clogged his throat.

That was weird. He'd never had a woman turn him down before. And not for a reason like Milla had given him. Hell, they could remain discreet at work.

Or was it something else? Something she hadn't admitted?

Could their lovemaking have disappointed her?

Kyle had never had to worry about whether things had been good for the lady in his bed. And he doubted that was the case now. But maybe things hadn't been as great as he'd thought they were.

He could ask her, he supposed. But she didn't seem to want to talk about it anymore. And he wasn't sure he wanted to, either.

Kyle Bingham didn't chase after a woman. Never had; never would.

It wasn't his style.

As Milla watched Kyle go, his white coat flapping in the summer breeze, tears welled in her eyes and the bitter taste of regret lingered in her mouth. She felt as though she'd thrown away the winning ticket to the lottery.

But a woman couldn't lose what she'd never really had.

Milla certainly didn't love Kyle Bingham, but he was the kind of man she could easily fall for, a man who had the power to hurt her. Deeply.

It was better this way.

Really.

But there had been an undeniable attraction between the two of them. Okay, there still was, on her part. And what was worse, the sex had been great. So great that it would probably haunt any relationship she might have in the future, since she doubted another man could measure up.

Still, there was more to a relationship than hot sex. At least, that was the rose-colored dream she clung to.

Milla wanted a man she could trust to love her, to make a lifetime commitment, to stick around long enough to have children and watch them grow up—unlike her own dad, who hadn't called or dropped her a line since the day he'd driven away.

Besides, she and Kyle *did* work together, at least until he finished his residency. And that only made things awkward. Unnecessarily complicated.

And as if that weren't enough, she still had that damned lawsuit hanging over her head, stealing her peace of mind.

No, letting Kyle go was the right thing to do.

But try as she might, she couldn't fight her grief as she watched his departure.

"You sure are pensive for such a sunny day."

Milla looked up to see Dr. Mari Bingham, director of the midwifery school and clinic. The attractive but unadorned physician seemed more serious and more thoughtful than usual.

Mari was not only the doctor who ran the clinic and women's health center, she was also a talented medical professional who'd taken an interest in Milla, mentoring her while in school. They'd developed a closeness during those years, a bond the doctor didn't seem to have with the other midwives. It wasn't as though the two women were friends, but they had an understanding, a professional respect for each other.

Milla managed a smile, in spite of her own heavy heart. "It *is* a pretty day, isn't it?"

Mari nodded. "How are things going?"

Milla figured Mari wanted to know how she was doing with the lawsuit. Again, she was reminded of the problems the charge of malpractice had brought upon the clinic, even if she hadn't been at fault. "I'm doing all right."

"I'd like you to talk to Lillith—Lily—Cunningham, who's handling PR for the clinic. She'll play a role in trial preparations, as well as controlling press coverage."

The trial.

Press coverage.

The unfairness of the lawsuit slapped Milla again. Why did this have to happen? What had she done to deserve the unfounded accusations?

"I'll work with the PR director," Milla said. "And, by the way, Kyle has agreed to testify on my behalf. He was the resident on call the night the Canfields brought the baby in."

Mari nodded. "I'm aware of that."

Kyle was also Mari's cousin, although they never socialized, as far as Milla knew. Maybe because of Kyle's illegitimacy. Still, she thought it was kind of…sad. Kyle having cousins, a family and all, and not being close.

Milla tried to keep her thoughts on the trial. "Kyle said the Canfields had bandaged the umbilicus."

"I'm aware of that, too." Mari appeared preoccupied, stressed.

As much as Milla admired the OB/GYN, she didn't ask what was weighing on the director's mind. She figured Mari would mention it, if she wanted Milla to know.

"By the way, I'm going to be interviewing the staff tomorrow," Mari said.

"Why?" Milla couldn't mask the fear in her voice and hoped her mentor hadn't noticed.

Mari offered a tired smile. "Nothing about the lawsuit. I just have a few questions I'd like to have answered."

Milla nodded, hoping she would say more. She didn't.

"If you'll excuse me," Mari said, "I have a meeting in ten minutes with Lily. I'll tell her you'll be speaking to her soon."

"All right." Milla gathered the remnants of her lunch and stood, watching as the doctor she'd grown to admire strode away.

Mari would be interviewing the staff? Why?

She'd said it didn't have anything to do with the malpractice suit. Thank goodness. But what questions did Mari have?

Were the interviews a routine procedure? Or was something other than the malpractice suit creating a problem for the clinic?

There were rumors circulating, although there might not be much truth in any of them. There'd been a noticeable rise in the number of drug-addicted mothers and babies in recent months. Illegal use of prescription drugs, apparently, was on the rise in the community. And from what Milla had heard, the sheriff's department was investigating a black market drug ring, which might or might not be connected to the Foster Clinic.

The drug in question was Orcadol, an effective and highly addictive medication used for relief of chronic pain or pain after surgery. Orcadol had become the latest rage on the streets of Merlyn County. Abusers referred to it as Orchid and often tried to get around the timed-release formula in the pill by crushing them, chewing, snorting or injecting it. In fact, Orcadol had become so popular that addicts and dealers had been known to attack pharmacies in neighboring communities with guns to obtain the drug.

Another piece of gossip was that Mari Bingham might be involved in the drug ring. But that was ridiculous. Milla knew the conscientious physician would never be a part of something like that.

Still, the investigation seemed to worry Mari, making her want to seek some answers.

Was that the reason for the staff interviews? To find out what might be going on under Dr. Mari Bingham's nose?

Or was it something else?

Milla would ask the director tomorrow, during her own interview. Because right now all she could focus on was the unfair accusation the Canfields had made.

Kyle said he would testify on her behalf.

Would he still? Had the end of their hot but brief love affair changed that?

Milla hoped not, but she really didn't know the

man very well. Didn't know if he could separate their personal problems from their professional relationship.

He'd been a considerate lover. Did that mean he would be a man of his word?

Or would his promise to testify disappear like a pickup barreling down a gravel drive in a cloud of dust?

The clinic staff went on high alert as Dr. Bingham interviewed each of her employees in the conference room, starting with maintenance and working her way through each orderly, nurse and midwife on the payroll.

Milla waited in the break room across the hall, drinking a cup of overbrewed coffee.

Whispers abounded throughout the clinic today, and everyone's curiosity was apparent.

"Has she called you in yet?" Milla asked Crystal Hendrix, who reached into the staff refrigerator and pulled out a brown bag that held a container of yogurt and a plastic spoon.

"Yes, just a few minutes ago." The young nurse with strawberry-blond hair and fine features wore a dark, somber expression, one that appeared too heavy for her to bear.

"Is something wrong?" Milla asked.

"I'm just worried about my son. He's...so young, only six..." Crystal paused, trying to put her obvious

concern into words. "He's visiting his dad in Ohio.
And I miss him so much."

At least the man spent time with his son, Milla
thought. A lot of divorced dads just drove off into the
sunset without looking back. She placed a hand on
Crystal's shoulder. "I'm sure your little boy is fine
and having a great time."

Crystal tried to smile, but her eyes bore a burden
that showed no sign of lifting. "I'm sure you're
right."

Then the nurse excused herself and walked down
the corridor that led outside.

Milla watched her go. Crystal had lost weight.
From worry and stress? It was hard to say. And now
that Milla thought about it, Crystal had been quieter
than usual.

Milla's heart went out to the single mom who
struggled to make a home for her young son. Maybe
Milla ought to invite Crystal to dinner, for some girl
talk. But with their schedules, and Milla's determination to spend more time with Dylan, she wasn't
sure when she'd find a free evening.

While Milla waited to be called for her interview,
the trouble she faced because of the Canfield charges
took a back seat to the problems facing her mentor.

Even without this investigation and Milla's malpractice suit, Mari Bingham had enough to worry
about. The development of her new research facility
had sparked a heated debate in town. The planned
facility would fund and implement research in infer-

tility, stem-cell experiments and other controversial procedures. It would also provide much-needed jobs to the area.

Mari didn't deserve the negative attention.

And neither did the Foster Clinic.

As Cecilia Mendoza stepped out of Mari's office and into the break room, she bore a smile that spoke of her recent happiness. Her upcoming marriage to Geoff Bingham, Mari's brother, was common knowledge.

"You're next," Cecilia said to Milla.

Milla stood and made her way into the conference room, then took a seat across the table.

Mari cut right to the chase. "You're aware of the fact that we've had an unusually high number of drug-addicted mothers and babies recently."

Milla nodded. She'd delivered two herself, and both had been heartbreaking. The one baby who had lived was still in the neonatal intensive care unit and would probably suffer the effects of its mother's drug use for years to come.

"The sheriff's department is investigating a black market drug ring," Mari added.

"It's been rumored that they're focusing their attention on the clinic," Milla said.

"Have you noticed anything unusual? Anything at all?"

Milla clicked her tongue and blew out a sigh. "I've been so wrapped up in my own worries, with this malpractice suit and all, I haven't paid much attention to anything other than my job.''

''I'd appreciate it if you'd keep your eyes open, now that we…or rather I…may be a suspect.''

Milla was struck by the absurdity of a suspicion like that. ''Anyone who knows you—''

''Neither my character nor my reputation seem to matter to some people.''

Milla doubted Mari spoke this freely to the other employees. And she appreciated the candor. ''Have you learned anything today?''

Mari sat back in her chair, crossed her arms and allowed a wry grin to surface. ''Yes. I learned that Cecelia is happily looking forward to her elopement. Crystal is worried about her son. And you're still concerned about the lawsuit. But other than that?'' The doctor slowly shook her head. ''No, I don't have anything solid.''

''But you're worried that the Orcadol might be coming from the clinic?''

Mari studied her, then said, ''I find it hard to believe, but yes.''

''I haven't noticed anything shady or out of the ordinary around here. So if the Orcadol is coming from the Foster Clinic, it would have to be an inside job.''

''That's what I'm afraid of.''

The possibility of one of Milla's co-workers being involved was unsettling. ''I hope you're wrong.''

''So do I.'' Mari stood, signaling the interview was

over. "I'd appreciate it if you kept this conversation confidential."

"Absolutely." Milla scooted her chair away from the table and stood. "I'll be more observant."

"Thank you."

Milla left the conference room, her stomach turning at the thought of anything illegal or underhanded going on at the Foster Clinic.

She glanced at her watch. Lunchtime. And even though she didn't particularly feel like eating, she needed to force something down.

Unfortunately, she'd slept late this morning and hadn't taken time to pack a lunch. She didn't have much cash in her purse, but there were a few dollars in the glove box of her car for emergencies.

She'd no more than stepped out of the clinic when Kyle Bingham approached, his stance hard, his expression fierce, like that of a fair-haired Viking who'd been wronged.

Her heart slipped into overdrive, as she caught sight of a fire in the blue eyes that carried both a promise and a challenge.

"We need to talk."

Chapter Five

We need to talk.

Hadn't Milla already told Kyle why things couldn't develop any further between them?

"Talk about what?" she asked.

"About the other night." A hard-edged glint in his eyes suggested she hadn't made herself clear.

"I'm not sure there's anything left to talk about." She tucked a strand of hair behind her ear.

"I don't think you were being completely truthful."

For goodness' sake, she'd been as honest with him as she'd been with herself. Or had she?

Deep inside, she was afraid Kyle would wiggle into her heart, then grow tired of her and leave, just like his father had left Aunt Connie and the others. Just like her own dad had abandoned her and her mom.

But she couldn't see any point in admitting that. It was bad enough admitting it to herself. "I'm not sure what you're getting at. But if you'd like to talk more, we can. But not now."

"I didn't mean here and now. We can talk later this evening, over dinner."

Dinner?

Another date?

Memories of their last night together rattled her to the bone, causing her heart to slam against her chest, her pulse rate to flutter, then soar. She envisioned another romantic evening, dining by candlelight. Making out in the parking lot. Touching, tasting, teasing.

Was that his intent? Did he hope for the repeat of the night they'd shared?

If so, she wasn't sure she could fight off the arousing effects he had on her, if she agreed to see him again.

A flood of heat washed over her, as she thought of sharing Kyle's bed, making love. Reaching the peak of pleasure, then collapsing in waves of release.

Her body begged for another chance to be his lover, but her conscience knew better. And not just because they worked together or because of his testimony. It was more than that, even though she wanted desperately to deny it. She was afraid of falling for him, of getting in too deep.

"I don't think going out with you is a good idea," she said.

"Even for dinner?" His brows furrowed. And when his gaze snagged hers, a hot, sexual awareness passed between them, proving both of their thoughts had traveled from dinner to bed.

"Did I do something wrong?" he asked.

Wrong? Heavens no. He'd done everything right, sexually and romantically speaking, of course.

Milla scanned her surroundings again, still not seeing anyone within hearing distance. "It was nice, Kyle."

"Nice?" He snapped out the words as though she'd slapped him. As though she'd devalued what they'd shared.

She hadn't meant to do that, but she hadn't wanted to stroke his ego, either. Something told her the good-looking doctor was cocky enough without extra adoration.

But he was obviously offended.

"I'm sorry. *Nice* wasn't the right adjective." She couldn't help the flush on her cheeks or the crooked grin that tugged her lips. "It was great, okay? But we made a mistake."

He merely stared, as though having a difficult time understanding her decision.

"Maybe after the lawsuit is settled," she began, backpedaling a bit, offering hope for the future. "The timing might be better."

"Yeah," Kyle said, a sarcastic tone apparent in his voice. "Maybe."

Then he turned on his heel and strode away, taking the "maybe" with him and leaving Milla with no sense of hope, no way to resurrect a romance with a man whose kiss had the power to rock her very foundation.

It was over.

And that was for the best.

Really.

Men like Kyle had their choice of women. Bright, beautiful, wealthy women. Classy women who would slide as easily in and out of his world as they did his bed.

What did he need with someone like Milla, someone content to spend the rest of her life in Merlyn County, Kentucky? And then there was her commitment to Dylan. Most bachelors didn't want to get involved with single mothers.

No, it made perfect sense to end things before they got carried away, before Milla got in so deep that a breakup would hurt her.

Yet a dark spirit of melancholy settled over her, nearly buckling her knees.

No more romantic, candlelight dinners. No more silent glances laden with desire. No more hungry kisses. No more passion-filled nights in Kyle's arms.

That was good, Milla reiterated. There really was no future between them. They were colleagues, and only temporary colleagues at that. Kyle was leaving in two years, returning to do research in Boston. Hadn't he made that clear?

The only thing debatable was the length of time their relationship would last, not the fact that it would eventually end.

Milla was just protecting herself from the inevitable.

The problem was, she didn't feel protected—or safe from heartbreak.

Letting him go had hurt, more than she'd expected.

But better *now* than later, she told herself, before she had time to make an emotional investment in the man.

It made perfect sense, yet a hard, dull ache in her heart suggested she'd invested something already. More than she'd realized.

She glanced in the direction Kyle had walked and spotted him in the parking lot. He didn't see her. Didn't even turn his head. She watched as he climbed in his BMW, revved the engine, backed out of his reserved space and sped off.

No gravel. No dust.

But the image of him driving away without looking back would stick with her for a long time to come.

Milla's rejection had wounded Kyle's pride. But he supposed that was understandable. In all the times he'd gone to bat, he'd never struck out with a woman before. Not after taking her to bed, anyway.

Nice? Had she really classified their lovemaking as nice?

Nah. He knew better than that—even though he'd had moments of doubt. The sex had been incredible, for both of them. Heck, he still had her scratch marks on his back to prove it.

Maybe Milla was flighty or relationship shy.

Now, wasn't that ironic? Kyle had never been one to make commitments. And he sure as hell wasn't looking for something semipermanent now.

So what was the problem? What had him so damn bothered? Had the blow of her rejection struck something else? Something more sensitive than his pride?

Nope. Impossible.

Kyle didn't allow women to get that close or to have that kind of hold on him. Still, the sting of her rebuff followed him like a dark shadow, not showing any signs of leaving. And as if that weren't enough, memories of their lovemaking had dogged him throughout the past couple of days and nights.

He'd tried his best to ignore the unwelcome thoughts, to shrug them off as inconsequential. Hell, a promising medical career meant far more to him than any lover ever would.

His sex life, as healthy as it was, had always been a secondary part of his life. A drizzle of icing on the cake, so to speak.

So why had this woman's lack of interest left him so edgy?

It was a mystery to him. And not one worth solving. So, trying his best to put Milla Johnson behind him, Kyle poured himself into his work.

Two days later, while making rounds, he stopped by the neonatal intensive care unit to check on Baby Elwood, a tough little girl who had been born weighing just barely a pound. Sometimes, when things got him down and he needed a boost, he came by to see her.

What a fighter.

So tiny, with the odds against her, she'd managed to flail her tiny arms in protest at being thrust into the cold, cruel world before her time, as her lungs struggled to draw breath.

Kyle had been the resident on call the night she'd been born, the night the midwife had requested medical backup.

Mrs. Elwood had been only twenty-six weeks along when her water broke. And an otherwise uneventful pregnancy suddenly became high risk. The neonatologist on call had been in surgery, assisting with a set of triplets that had arrived two months earlier than expected. So Kyle stepped in until he'd been relieved by someone who specialized in micropreemies.

The Elwood baby was no longer his patient, but he often stopped to check on her. He'd always favored underdogs—probably because he'd felt like one as a kid. And it pleased him to see the progress she'd made. Although not out of the woods, she'd nearly doubled her weight and seemed to be doing well.

When Kyle entered the NICU, he saw Milla standing over the Elwood baby and his heart ricocheted against the wall of his chest. He didn't know why it surprised him to see her there. Milla had been the midwife who'd brought the mother to the hospital. The midwife who'd stayed through the night and into the next day, offering support to the frightened parents.

Apparently, the baby had touched her, too.

For a moment Kyle wanted to turn around, to walk out, to try his best to ignore the discomfort he felt at seeing Milla again. The woman who'd worked some kind of sexual magic on him, then dumped him.

Yeah. That's what it was. Sex, pure and simple. That was the hold she had on him.

Milla took a deep breath, then spoke. "I just stopped by to check on her, to see how she's doing."

"She's holding her own, from what I understand."

Milla nodded, then softly placed a hand on the incubator, as though sending loving vibes through the plastic barrier that protected the baby. "They named her Catherine Grace."

Kyle watched Milla for a moment, watched her study the tiny infant whose fingers hadn't been much bigger than grains of rice when she'd been born.

In spite of his determination to remain unaffected by Milla's presence, by the thoughts behind the woman, he couldn't help his curiosity. "How often do you come to see her?"

He figured this wasn't the first time. He'd felt some kind of bond to the baby; she probably had, too.

"Once a week or so. Her parents try hard to make sure someone is with her as often as possible, but today they had to go to their six-year-old son's T-ball game. So I volunteered to stop by in their place."

"Are you friends with the Elwoods?" Kyle asked.

"Not really." Her eyes sought his and locked on something deep inside. "I can't explain it."

Compassion, he suspected. And dedication. The traits that made her a good midwife. And a good person, no doubt.

For a moment Kyle reevaluated his previous determination—that the attraction he felt for Milla was based on lust and sex. It was all that and more, he supposed.

Sure, memories of her sweet taste and the feel of her in his arms remained dangerously close to the surface, but he found Milla Johnson appealing, intriguing.

But so what?

She'd made herself clear. She didn't want anything to do with him. And that was just fine with him.

No problem.

Before Kyle could say any more, before he could walk away as though he'd merely wandered into NICU without a purpose, Milla excused herself, then stepped out of the room.

His heart jumped, did a belly flop, then roared to life.

Damn it. How could just talking to her, being near her, do that to him? The doe-eyed brunette stirred his blood more than he cared to admit, but he wasn't going to chase after her. No way.

Kyle had given up trying to prove himself years ago, not to people who didn't give a damn about him, anyway.

Everything he'd accomplished, he'd done on his own—in spite of a notorious tie to the legitimate branch of the Bingham family.

Kyle had become a doctor because he'd wanted to. It was as simple as that. He'd mapped out his life, and his plans didn't include being part of the Binghams or this hospital.

He didn't have any attachments to Merlyn County, nor did he want any. And other than his mother, Kyle didn't feel any sense of loyalty toward anyone.

Yet whatever it was that drew him to Milla Johnson left him perplexed and slightly unbalanced.

Cursing his weakness under his breath, he returned to the E.R., where he belonged.

Milla had the next Sunday off work, so she decided to make good on her promise and spend time with Dylan.

When she suggested a movie, the boy's eyes widened and his mouth dropped open. "No kidding?"

How long had it been since she'd spent quality time with him?

A bit longer than she could remember, she supposed. But she'd been busy with school, and now she was trying to get her practice off the ground—each of them good excuses in their own right. Yet a twinge of guilt tweaked her heart, and she made up her mind to find more time for him. Quality time.

And if that meant she had to actually block out a space on her pocket calendar, she'd do just that.

"No kidding," she said. "You and I need to start spending more time together. That's what mothers and sons do."

Dylan wrapped his arms around her and gave her a kid-size squeeze that reached her soul. Then he took off to find his shoes and his favorite baseball cap.

Minutes later they drove to the Bijou, an old-style movie theater located on Main, about three blocks down from Melinda's. Housed in a stately, white stucco building, the Bijou boasted a big, old-fashioned marquee with flashing lights that advertised the latest Tom Hanks flick, which would show tonight. During the long, lazy days of summer, the theater offered family classics as afternoon matinees. Today's fare was the Disney movie, *Old Yeller.*

Milla hadn't been to a movie in years, in part because she hadn't had time—or the extra money. But she and Dylan would splurge this afternoon. And later, after the movie, they'd stop by May's Dairy Hut and get a double-dip ice-cream cone.

Before sliding out of the car, Dylan said, "Aunt Sharon got all weird when I called you Mom. You think that's because she doesn't want to be my grandma?"

"I'm sure it only surprised her." Milla probably

should have discussed the issue with her mother so the poor woman could have been prepared when Dylan brought up the subject, but it had slipped her mind. "Our moms were sisters, and they loved each other a lot. Your aunt Sharon always gets kind of sad and melancholy whenever she thinks about her sister."

"Yeah," Dylan said. "Aunt Sharon sometimes gets kind of grumpy and weird like that, especially when she tries to boss you around and it doesn't work."

Was it that obvious? Milla couldn't keep a grin from tugging at her lips. "Sometimes she forgets that I'm an adult with a mind of my own."

"Yeah. But she always gives in."

Well, not always. But that didn't mean they couldn't compromise, when necessary.

Milla chuckled at the child's insight into his aunt's moods. "She usually gives in when she knows I'm right. And that's why she'll be okay with our new relationship, once she gets used to the idea. I won't let you forget your real mother, just because I'm your mom now."

As they made their way to the theater ticket office, Dylan asked, "Can I give the lady the money?"

"Sure." Milla pulled a twenty from the wallet in her purse and handed it to him.

"Can we get popcorn and sodas, too?"

"You bet."

As Dylan ran ahead, Milla took her time, studying

the movie posters that advertised the coming attractions. When she turned to follow Dylan, she caught sight of a couple strolling down the street.

Kyle.

And another woman.

Milla's breath caught, and her pulse darn near stopped. The pretty woman looked familiar. Who was she?

As the couple approached, the woman slipped an arm through his and smiled proudly. Recognition dawned.

Kyle was with the cute blond nurse who worked on the pediatric floor. Her name was Kristin something. Or maybe it was Kelly.

"Hi," the shapely blonde said, a forty-watt smile proclaiming her thrill to be seen on Dr. Bingham's arm.

Kyle merely nodded, an air of indifference in his stance and manner.

Milla tried to shrug off her disappointment, to appear cordial and professional when her tummy was doing flip-flops and her heart was pounding like crazy. "Hello."

"Going to a movie?" Kristin or Kelly asked.

"Yes, with my—" Milla, momentarily forgetting, nearly said cousin, until Dylan walked up and handed her a ticket. He smiled broadly, his happiness at spending the day with her obvious.

Milla swallowed the awkwardness of seeing Kyle

with another woman and continued, "This is my son, and we're going to see a matinee."

Kyle seemed to assess the boy, taking in his light-colored hair, his big blue eyes, his dimpled smile. Looking for a family resemblance, she assumed, and probably finding his half brother to look a lot like him.

Then Kyle turned his gaze on Milla, sending her senses reeling and setting her nerves on end.

Get over it, she commanded, with little effect. Her body seemed to have a mind of its own when it came to Kyle.

"Dylan, this is Dr. Bingham and—" Milla paused again, then looked at the woman. "I'm sorry, but I've forgotten your name."

"Karla," the woman said, reaching out a hand to Dylan.

Your son? Kyle's expression seemed to ask. *What's going on?*

"It's not official yet," Milla said, "but I'm going to adopt Dylan."

Kyle smiled at the boy and shook his hand in greeting, then, without granting Milla the same warmth, he said, "If you'll excuse us, we need to go."

Where? Milla wanted to ask. Where are you two going? What are you up to? Are you lovers? But she held her tongue and nodded, trying desperately to ignore the pounding in her chest, the blood racing through her veins. The godawful lump in her throat.

What was wrong with her?

She watched Kyle and Karla continue on their way. Watched Kyle saunter down the street with the well-endowed blonde clutching his arm. The pretty nurse turned and flashed the handsome doctor a dazzling smile.

An ache settled deep in Milla's heart. She wanted to backpedal, to turn the clock back a week. But it was too late. She'd made a mistake. Like a broken-hearted child who didn't know what was best for her, Milla wanted to throw herself on the sidewalk and kick her feet in frustration, in disappointment.

How could Kyle's coming and going affect her like that?

"Hey, Mom," Dylan said. "The movie is going to start without us."

"You're right. Sorry for dawdling." She took the ticket from the boy's hand and followed him into the red-carpeted theater.

Knock it off, she told herself. You set the rules, didn't you? So now it's time to abide by them.

Still, Milla felt hollow and alone.

It hurt to see Kyle with someone else. To have him pass her on the street as though she were a flickering light on a marquee.

But letting the dapper doctor go was for the best.

Really, it was.

"Have you seen this movie before?" Dylan asked.

"I read the book," Milla said, realizing they were heading for a tearjerker.

Old Yeller would get rabies, trying to protect his

family, and he wouldn't live through the movie. The boy who loved him would have to put him out of his misery.

Milla followed Dylan into the movie theater, feeling like the kid who had to shoot the big yellow dog he'd grown to love.

Chapter Six

Two weeks later, bright and early on a Wednesday morning, Milla entered the only bathroom in the apartment, carrying a small brown bag in her hand and a nagging fear in her heart.

. Of course, her fear might be unwarranted, but she needed to know for sure. And there was no need to start any unnecessary rumors at the lab.

Once inside the windowless room, she flipped on the light switch, setting off the automatic fan that roared to life. Then, after locking the door and securing her privacy, she blew out a troubled sigh.

The pale yellow walls seemed to close in on her as she opened the bag and pulled out the home pregnancy test she'd purchased in town yesterday.

Her hands shook as she tore open the box, carefully read the instructions and then diligently followed each step.

Once she'd finished, she looked upward, searching the ceiling for a glimpse of heaven, a line of divine communication.

"Please," she prayed. "Don't let me be pregnant. Not now."

Milla had always wanted to feel the first fluttering movements of a baby in her womb, to experience the birth of her own tiny son or daughter, but the timing couldn't be worse.

Surely she hadn't gotten pregnant. She and Kyle had used protection. But their efforts might have grown careless as their desire raged on. Would she suffer the natural consequences of a night of thoughtless passion?

Maybe the fear that now bordered on panic was unfounded.

Her period was late, but that could certainly be caused by stress. And she definitely had plenty to worry about: the lawsuit and the possibility that a black market drug ring was operating out of the clinic.

And then there were those jumbled feelings she had for Kyle—a man she shouldn't have gotten involved with in the first place, a man whose musky, sea-breezy scent, vibrant blue eyes and crooked smile haunted her dreams.

She blew out a shaky sigh, closed the lid to the toilet and sat down. Staring at the plastic kit, she waited, the seconds plunking away like a funeral dirge playing an ode to life as she once knew it.

She glanced at the scruffy yellow slippers on her feet, her eyes traveling to the gray and pink speckles in the worn, linoleum flooring.

How much longer would it take? She checked her watch, silently rejoicing when the required minutes had finally passed.

"Okay," she whispered against the roar of the fan and the throbbing pulse pounding in her ears. "Time for the moment of truth."

She studied the small, plastic apparatus that held her future, watched as a telltale pink dot formed ever so slowly.

She was pregnant.

With Kyle Bingham's baby.

Her heart sank into the dank, empty pit of her stomach, as the ramifications settled over her.

The Canfields and their attorney would have a field day if they ever caught wind of this. And Mari Bingham, the mentor she respected, was sure to be disappointed by what could only be considered unprofessional behavior. And Milla's promising career, once heading upward, would take a nosedive when the news leaked out.

A rap sounded at the door, then her mother's voice asked, "Milla, are you in there?"

Suddenly reminded of the problems she would face at home, she uttered a subdued and nearly silent "Oh, boy" and blew out a sigh. Her mother was going to flip, especially if she knew Milla was pregnant with Billy Bingham's grandchild.

"I'll be out in a minute, Mom." As soon as I gather my wits. As soon as I sort through what few options I have available.

"Breakfast is ready," her mom added in a voice that sounded far more chipper than anyone had a right to be on a day like this. "We're having hotcakes this morning—Dylan's favorite."

Good. Let Dylan have her share. Milla couldn't even think of eating. A wave of nervousness swept through her, settling in her tummy. It was probably too early for morning sickness, but her stomach didn't know that, as it tossed and turned, threatening to up-chuck at any moment.

She glanced in the bathroom mirror and caught sight of a pale, wan woman with stringy, uncombed hair peering hopelessly back at her. Scared. Nervous. And laden with guilt.

What in heaven's name would she tell Kyle? And how would he react?

A handsome, sought-after bachelor like him, with a big-city future before him, wouldn't want to be tied down—not to a mountain community in Kentucky, not to a wife. And certainly not to a baby.

Would Kyle be angry when she told him? Uncaring? Distant? All of the above?

Milla wanted to hoard the news as long as possible, to avoid facing the consequences.

For goodness' sake, Kyle didn't even know she existed. Not anymore. Not after she'd let him know things were over between them.

Of course, ending things had been her decision— not his. But even if she hadn't told him their short-lived relationship was over, he probably would have grown tired of her and moved on to another woman.

Like he'd already moved on to Karla, Milla reminded herself.

An image of the smiling, bright-eyed blond nurse who'd proudly stood at Kyle's side came to mind. A woman who made no secret of her attraction to the handsome doctor, or of her interest in taking their professional relationship to a romantic level. A sexual level.

The thought of anyone else in Kyle's arms, in his bed, tore at Milla's heart, making her realize it had been more than hormones involved in all of this, more than lust.

Okay. She had to admit she was infatuated with the man, to say the least. Otherwise it wouldn't hurt so bad to think of Kyle with someone new.

Well, Milla had better get used to seeing other women with Kyle. He probably changed dates as often as he changed his socks. At least, that's the scuttlebutt she'd recently heard through the midwifery grapevine.

She'd told herself she didn't care about Kyle's reputation with the ladies, that she'd merely been flattered by his attention. That she'd been curious, had that curiosity satisfied in a very pleasant way, then gotten out of the situation before it was too late.

But that wasn't entirely true. She hadn't gotten out in time. And look at her now. She was in way too deep—way over her head.

And not just because she was pregnant.

Milla was helplessly infatuated with her baby's father, a man who no longer gave a hoot about her.

Could her life get any more complicated than this?

Probably not.

And there was no one to blame but herself.

Kyle couldn't believe he'd done something so...so uncharacteristically noble and moral.

When his one and only lunch date with Karla had ended, he'd taken her home—to her house—even though by any standards, the day was still young and promising. But for some crazy reason, he wanted to be alone.

He hadn't been sure why. Maybe because seeing Milla at the Bijou had set off a barrage of memories in his head, reminding him of what he'd once tasted and could no longer look forward to. Or maybe Karla didn't set his blood pumping the way Milla did.

As he'd stood with Karla on her porch, the pretty blonde slid him a sultry smile. "I had a great time, but it's too soon to call it a day."

The sun still blazed in the afternoon sky, and he supposed she was right, but he didn't feel the compulsion to drag things out and play the game. Not even when Karla wrapped her arms around his neck, pressed her size-D breasts against his chest, leaned into him and rubbed herself against him, coaxing him to reconsider calling it a day.

There'd been no question about what Karla had in mind, but for some unexplained reason, nothing seemed to be happening on his side of the embrace.

She might not have suspected his disinterest, because she'd given him one of those why-don't-we-spend-the-afternoon-getting-naked kisses, urging his mouth to open, his tongue to mate.

Kyle had actually hoped her efforts would work, that the willing nurse would trigger a convenient and welcome case of sexual amnesia to wipe Milla's image, her touch and her taste from his mind.

But it hadn't worked.

Hunger had been missing from the kiss, and so had heat. On his part, at least.

"Come inside," she'd purred, words dripping with a hot, sexual come-on.

It was the kind of offer he rarely turned down, yet he'd stepped back and broken contact. The sobering movement had surprised them both.

"I've got an early day tomorrow," he'd told her by way of an excuse. But in actuality, he feared Milla's kiss had come between them, something he wasn't at all happy to admit.

"Is something wrong?" Karla had asked, a little-girl pout on her face.

Hell, yes, there was something wrong, although he

wasn't exactly sure what it was. The fact that Karla did nothing for him was a starter. It was also reason enough not to consider her let's-get-naked offer. For cripe's sake, what if he couldn't perform? It happened to guys sometimes. Never him, though. And he wasn't about to risk it.

"I've got a lot of work to do at home before it gets dark," he'd told her. "So, I'd better take a rain check."

"Okay," Karla had said. "But see that you do. You won't be sorry."

He'd flashed her a smile, then turned and walked away, feeling as though he'd escaped.

After sliding into the seat of his BMW, he'd pondered what had just transpired.

Kyle Bingham had graciously turned down the opportunity to have sex with a very willing, very attractive nurse. And even now, after the fact, it didn't quite seem normal. Or healthy.

He'd never reacted like that before. In fact, he'd never found an attractive woman unappealing before.

Hell, he certainly didn't need to score with every woman he went out with. What did it matter if he narrowed the playing field a little? Being more selective didn't mean he was the kind of guy looking to settle down with just one woman. There was too damn much of his footloose, playboy dad in him, he supposed.

As much as Kyle had hated growing up in Billy Bingham's shadow, he'd always seemed to be more like his dad than any of the others—and not just in looks. Was it a genetic predisposition? As a kid, he'd heard comments like, "The apple doesn't fall far from the tree."

Or was it something else? Some stupid subconscious attempt to emulate the man who'd fathered him?

Who was the real Kyle Bingham? A rebellious bad boy like his dad? Or only a Billy Bingham wannabe, spawned by an angry, hurting boy who'd wanted a father more than anything in the world?

He supposed it really didn't matter. He just knew that he wasn't cut out to be a family man.

What the heck did he know about being a husband or father? There'd never been a man in his life. Hell, his mother had never even dated, not that he could remember.

He wasn't going to psychoanalyze himself, though. What was the use? He was happy with his life. Why stir up things that didn't matter anymore?

But maybe there was some other psychological stuff at work here, too, making him focus on one woman in particular.

Maybe Milla being unattainable had gained his interest, holding him in some kind of sexual death grip. Maybe that's why he couldn't shake her image, her floral, spring-garden scent.

He'd told himself that one night with her was all he needed. But that no longer seemed to be the case. Maybe, rather than avoiding her and acting aloof, he needed to pursue her again—to sate himself of her touch, of her scent. Then he could get over her and get on with his life.

Kyle wouldn't make any promises or commitments to her—he wasn't that kind of guy. But making amends might do both him and Milla a lot of good.

Hadn't she mentioned something about taking up where they left off, after the trial was over?

Well, why wait? They could keep things quiet and on the sly. People didn't need to know they were dating. And they didn't even need to date. Making love one more time might be all he needed get her out of his system.

Otherwise, his once-active love life might take a beating—something he didn't need.

So where to start?

He'd seen Milla's car in the parking lot today, which meant she was probably working. Now all he needed was an excuse to head over to the clinic.

His dad might have been a lousy father, but he did have a certain charm with the ladies, something Kyle had inherited.

It would only be a matter of time before Milla realized she'd made a mistake by walking out on him.

Milla glanced up from the chart she'd been studying as she walked along the main hallway in the Janice Foster Clinic. She saw Mari Bingham approach.

Just the person Milla needed to talk to. "Doctor, do you have a minute?"

"Sure." Mari paused, giving Milla her undivided attention.

"I have a patient in her twenty-third week, with increasing blood-sugar levels. I'd like you to look over the lab results, but I think it's a case of gestational diabetes."

Mari studied the numbers, then nodded. "I agree."

It was standard procedure for the Foster Clinic midwives to refer any of their high-risk patients to one of the obstetricians on staff. And that was Milla's intention in this case.

Mari reached into her lab coat and withdrew a plastic container of tiny mints. She offered one to Milla. "Would you like some?"

"No, thanks."

Mari popped two in her own mouth, then said, "Why don't you have your patient talk to scheduling and set up an appointment with me?"

"I'll do that."

Before Mari could continue on her way, a lab tech stopped her. "Excuse me, Dr. Bingham, but I have those results you wanted."

"Thank you." Mari took the file, then glanced at the paperwork and sighed heavily.

"Is something wrong?" Milla asked.

Mari scanned the hallway where she and Milla stood. Finding it empty, she still lowered her voice. "One of our surgery patients had an allergic reaction to the Orcadol we gave her. She's had Orcadol in the past, with no side effects."

"What are you thinking?" Milla asked, aware of the concern that particular drug aroused.

"I think, to be on the safe side, it's time to send a sample of our Orcadol to the lab."

Was Mari wondering whether the patient had been given something else?

Milla's gut clenched at the thought that someone might have replaced the Orcadol with another drug—something the patient had been allergic to.

"I hope your concern is unfounded."

"So do I." Then Mari turned and continued on her way down the hall.

Milla's stomach rumbled, reminding her she hadn't eaten in a while, not since she'd had half of a pancake at breakfast. She glanced at her wristwatch—one-twenty-five. No wonder. She'd nearly worked through lunch again—not a good idea, these days. Hadn't she stressed the importance of regular, nutritious meals to her pregnant patients?

She'd better take her own advice.

Since she'd planned to use her lunch hour to run some errands, one of which was to pick up some pre-natal vitamins at the drugstore, she would have to eat her sandwich in the car.

She didn't have much time to spare, so she grabbed her purse out of her locker and dashed out of the clinic.

The sun burned brightly in the afternoon sky, promising a lazy summer day. Too bad she didn't have time to sit outside and enjoy it.

As she made her way down the sidewalk, a familiar voice called out. A voice that settled over her like a heated cloak of crushed velvet. "Just the lady I wanted to see."

Kyle Bingham stood before her like a fair-haired Greek god, sunlight glistening off the gold strands in his hair.

Every fiber of her being stood on end, alive with heightened awareness. Her senses reeled, and her curiosity mounted. As much as she wanted to hear what he had to say, now wasn't a good time to talk.

"I need to run some errands," she said.

Knowledge of the baby they'd created hovered around her, creating a push-pull effect, begging her to hear him out, while urging her to find a good excuse to quickly disappear.

Before he could respond, her cell phone rang.

"Excuse me," she told him, appreciating the distraction.

"Hello."

"Ms. Johnson?" a male voice asked.

"Yes."

"This is Mr. Rick, the director of the Daniel Boone Kid's Club."

Oh, no. Dylan. "Is something wrong?"

Of course there was. The man wouldn't call to chat. All kinds of scary thoughts ran through her mind.

"There was another fight."

Her face must have contorted, because Kyle studied

her expression, watching intently as she listened to the man's words.

"I warned both boys, but it didn't seem to help. Now I have to make good on my threat to send them both home for a few days."

"Did anyone get hurt?" she asked.

"Dylan lost a tooth in the scuffle, but it was already loose, or so he said."

"I'll be right there." Without thinking of her audience, Milla rolled her eyes and clicked her tongue as she ended the call.

"Is Dylan all right?" Kyle asked.

It surprised her that he remembered the boy's name, although she wasn't entirely sure why it would. They were, after all, half brothers. And she'd spotted Kyle's interest in Dylan outside the Bijou.

"Yes, he's all right. But this is the third fight he's had at day camp this month. And now he and the other boy are being suspended for a few days."

"Who did he fight with?" Kyle asked.

"Kirk Brower. Or better known as Kirk the Jerk—the stupidest kid in the whole world."

"I've known a few kids who could have given Kirk the Jerk a run for his money." Kyle's eyes lit up with mirth, but Milla found it hard to share his humor. Dylan's problems were beginning to wear on her.

"Hey," Kyle said, placing a hand on her shoulder, offering comfort she hadn't expected. "You're really worried about him, aren't you?"

"Yes. The Brower boy has been teasing him about

not having parents. About—'' she took a deep breath, then finished the words, hoping they wouldn't offend Kyle ''—about being one of Billy's brats.''

One of Billy's brats. Kyle's eyes narrowed, his lips tightened. He didn't blame Dylan for fighting or for wanting to make the taunts stop. Kyle had pummeled more than his share of loudmouthed jerks, until he'd made a name for himself as a hard-ass. And eventually the teasing had stopped.

Kyle supposed that wasn't the kind of attitude he should have as an adult, as a competent pediatrician, but the poor kid's plight had stirred up some painful memories. He'd lived through his own share of bruised knuckles and black eyes, fighting some of the same kinds of taunts.

''Kids can be cruel,'' Milla said.

Cruel? They could be brutal. And so could some adults. ''I'd like to talk to Dylan, if that's okay.''

Milla's eyes widened, brightened. ''Really?''

Yeah, really. The kid was suffering from some of the same crap Kyle'd had to deal with. It had been tough growing up as one of Billy's bastards. But it wasn't something he talked about.

Still he felt for the kid and wondered if he might be able to give Dylan some emotional support, something no one had been able to offer Kyle. ''Maybe I can take him fishing. Or something like that.''

She seemed to struggle with his offer, but then the furrow on her brow disappeared and her expression softened. ''That would be great. Raising little boys is a bit out of my league. I never had any brothers, and my dad…well, he wasn't around much.''

Kyle hadn't had a man around the house, either, and he sure didn't plan on raising any kids of his own. But he sympathized with the boy—his half brother— more than he cared to admit.

''I could take him out to Ginman's Lake next weekend.'' Kyle wasn't sure why he'd suggested a trip to the lake. All he knew was that he felt sorry for the kid.

Her eyes sparkled in a way he hadn't noticed, not since sitting across the table with her at Melinda's. ''I'm sure he would love it. Thank you for offering to take him.''

''Maybe you can go with us, too.'' Kyle didn't think he could be so lucky, not after she'd put the kibosh on a relationship with him. But when her face lit up, he felt like a kid up at bat.

''Sure,'' she said. ''I can work it out. Just let me know when.''

''How about Saturday morning. Around ten?''

''I'll have to check my schedule, but that should work out. I'll give you a call to confirm. Then we'll meet you there.''

Again, Milla wanted to be in control, to have her own car. Or maybe she just didn't want him knowing where she lived. The thought that her mother might hold his parentage against him came to mind.

He tried to shrug off the old pain, the humiliation at being labeled. ''Great.''

She flashed him a dimpled smile that nearly knocked him to his knees, then took off with a spring to her step.

Had she changed her mind about them seeing each other again? On a personal level?

For some reason, as Kyle watched Milla go, he felt as though he stood at home plate with a full count and bases loaded.

Well, score one for the home team.

Kyle didn't intend to strike out.

Chapter Seven

Milla woke on Saturday morning with a rush of anticipation. She was looking forward to seeing Kyle today, in a casual, outdoor setting.

Away from the hospital and gossip.

She felt like a giddy schoolgirl with a crush on the new boy in school, but she tried to put a lid on her excitement. Getting involved with him right now still wasn't a good idea. And even if the lawsuit were no longer an issue, Kyle had moved on to someone new.

The only reason Milla had agreed to go to the lake with Kyle was so Dylan could spend some time with the man who was his brother. She certainly didn't harbor any fantasies of renewing their affair.

Then why not let them go alone? her conscience asked.

The question took her aback, and she scrambled for an answer.

Because Dylan didn't know Kyle. Because the boy could sometimes be shy in new situations. Because her presence would make things easier for everyone.

That's why.

From the moment she'd mentioned going to the lake with her friend, Dylan began counting the days. And it pleased her to see the boy happy.

She was going with them for Dylan's sake, she reminded herself. And not because of some silly crush on a doctor who was too classy and too good-looking for his own good. Besides, Kyle had already set his sights on Karla. Hadn't he?

The realization hurt, even though she knew his reputation.

"Hey, Mom?" Dylan asked. "Can I take my baseball? And my bat and mitt? And maybe—"

Milla laughed. "Slow down, slugger. Dr. Bingham's going to bring fishing gear, so there's no need for you to take anything.

"Maybe just my football? Or a Frisbee?"

She understood Dylan wanting to be prepared. Ginman's Lake was a popular recreational spot that stretched the length of a small valley, with lots of grassy spots for picnics or for kids to run and play.

In fact, Milla probably should bring along a book to read. Fishing didn't interest her. Besides, this was Dylan's day to spend with Kyle. She was merely along for the ride. Her plan was to help break the ice, then sit back and let things unfold naturally.

She looked at Dylan, her son, and smiled. She spotted the happiness in his bright smile. She also saw that he hadn't combed his hair after his morning shower.

An awkward spike at the crown of his head stood on end, and she brushed her hand against it, trying to get it to stay down. It remained standing.

"Why don't you go wet your hair down again?" she asked. "It dried before you combed it, so now it looks messy."

"It's okay, Mom. I'm going to wear my hat." He ran a hand across his head, then plopped his red baseball cap on top.

Milla opened her mouth to insist, then thought better of it. What would it hurt? She didn't want to be a fussy mother. Besides, there would be bigger issues in the future, issues she wouldn't back down on.

"All right. And if you want to take your football, go ahead. But don't dawdle. It's time to go, and you can help me carry things to the car."

"What kind of things?"

"I've packed us a lunch, as well as drinks and some snacks."

"Can we please take some junk food and stuff that's not good for us?" the boy asked.

"Of course not." A grin tugged at her lips. "What kind of mom would I be if I didn't pack healthy food and treats?"

"A cool mom," Dylan said, but he smiled just the same. "I'll go get my football."

As the boy dashed off, Milla realized she should tell her mother they were leaving. The poor woman hadn't slept well last night and had stayed in bed longer than usual.

Milla poked her head into their shared room, where the blinds had shut out most of the morning light. "Dylan and I are taking off now."

"Okay," her mom said, sitting up in bed and running a hand through her dark, sleep-tousled hair. "I know you probably mentioned it before, but who did you say you were going with?"

"One of the doctors from the hospital." Milla's cheeks warmed. Had they turned red? Heated by deceit?

Oh, for goodness' sake. She hadn't lied. Not really. If her mom asked for more details or for a name, she'd give it to her. She would also listen to 101 reasons why she shouldn't trust a Bingham and why Kyle was probably just like his father. And after listening, she would take Dylan to the lake, anyway.

Still, the fact that Milla was being a little sneaky didn't sit well with her. But neither did the idea of having any kind of confrontation with her mother before meeting with Kyle. Milla didn't want anything to put a damper on Dylan's day.

Or, to be honest, on hers.

"Have fun, honey."

"We will," Milla said, before softly closing the door.

Moments later, she and Dylan climbed into her car and drove to the lake, a few miles outside of town, where a colorful array of wildflowers dotted the green hillsides. Milla hadn't traveled much, but she couldn't imagine a more beautiful place to live. She loved Merlyn County, Kentucky.

As they approached the parklike grounds that surrounded the lake, many people—probably families—had already gathered. A somber mood settled over Milla, in spite of her son's lighthearted jabber.

She hadn't mentioned to Dylan that Kyle was his half brother, and now she wondered whether she should have. But for some reason it seemed like something Kyle should tell him. Not something she should reveal.

"This sure is a big place," Dylan said, scanning the crowded lakeside grounds. "How are we going to find him?"

"He'll meet us by the boathouse," she said.

The idea of Kyle standing them up knotted Milla's stomach. She didn't want to see Dylan disappointed, although she understood the demands of the medical profession.

There was always the chance that something unexpected might have come up, that Kyle might have had an emergency. Any number of excuses could have kept him away. Surely he would have called had his plans changed.

When she'd talked to him on the phone yesterday and confirmed their date…or rather, their outing, he'd volunteered to pick them up. And she'd insisted on meeting him.

It was better that way.

Why stir up things at home before he arrived? There was plenty of time to tell her mother that one of the Binghams had taken an interest in Dylan.

"Isn't that your doctor friend?" Dylan asked, pointing to Kyle. "He's not all dressed up like before, but it looks like him."

Kyle stood by his black BMW, wearing a pair of khaki shorts and a bright, multicolored shirt. He flashed them both a smile, then pulled fishing gear out of his trunk.

With her eyes on Dr. Hottie, Milla failed to brake in time and the car hit the concrete block at the edge of the parking space, causing her and Dylan to lurch forward, along with the car.

"Dammit," she muttered, regretting the word the moment she remembered Dylan was sitting in the back seat.

"Hey," Dylan said, ignoring her inappropriate outburst. "You need driving lessons."

Milla didn't respond. Instead, she took a quick peek in the rearview mirror to see if her klutzy attempt to gawk-and-park had been noticed.

A crooked grin on the dashing doctor's face was answer enough.

Great. She fought the urge to look in the mirror

and check her hair and lipstick. For goodness' sake, after the botched-up job of parking, it seemed kind of silly to primp so she would make a good impression. It was too late for that.

"Okay, Dylan. We're here."

As she'd expected, the boy who'd once been bouncing off the walls at home, eager for Saturday to come so they could go to the lake, remained in his seat. "I feel kind of...you know...weird."

So did Milla, but she refused to give in to the awkward feeling. "Dr. Bingham is looking forward to spending time with you. He likes kids."

Her words slammed against her heart. Did Kyle like kids? She assumed so, since he had chosen pediatrics as a specialty.

Of course, he *had* mentioned going into research, after his residency, which meant he didn't plan to work with children per se.

"Come on," she told Dylan. "Let's not keep the doctor waiting."

Kyle watched as Milla climbed from the car. She wore a pair of pink shorts and a white blouse, nothing stylish or designed to entice a healthy libido. Still, the sight made his blood pump in all the right places.

When she reached across the steering column and pulled out a big straw bag from the passenger side of the front seat, he couldn't keep from admiring the perfectly shaped legs that had once wrapped around him, urging him on.

Did she have those kinds of thoughts about him? He hoped so, because he had every intention of having those dynamite legs wrapped around him again.

"Thanks for inviting us," she said, closing the car door. "We've been looking forward to spending some time in the sun."

Yeah, well, he'd been looking forward to a day at the lake, too. In part, because he wanted to see her again, without the subdued expression she'd worn since she'd left his house after that night of great sex. And he wanted to see her away from the clinic or hospital, places where she might be reminded of reasons why they shouldn't see each other.

"I packed a lunch, in case we get hungry." She opened the rear door and pulled out a beat-up blue-and-white ice chest from the back seat.

"Let me get that for you." Kyle handed Dylan the fishing poles, then took the insulated chest from Milla. "I figured we'd pick up something at the snack bar, but a homemade lunch sounds better."

A warm summer breeze blew a strand of hair across her face, and she tucked it behind an ear and smiled. She had a sweet, wholesome look about her, nothing flashy, yet he found himself staring, drinking in her dimpled grin and laughing eyes.

Who would have thought those whiskey-colored orbs held a passionate fire that could turn a man inside out?

Kyle muttered a curse under his breath. Thinking

about the night they'd spent together wasn't going to do him one bit of good. Not today.

Not when he needed to focus on the boy. No one understood the difficulty of growing up as one of Billy's brats more than Kyle. And he wished there was something he could do to make it up to the kid.

"Are you ready to see if the fish are biting?" Kyle asked him.

Dylan nodded.

"How about you?" he asked Milla.

She patted the straw bag she carried and smiled. "I brought along a book."

"That's 'cause she's a girl," Dylan explained.

As if Kyle hadn't noticed. But Milla was the kind of girl that made a guy look forward to getting a good case of cooties.

Milla spread out a worn, yellow blanket, then set up a campsite of sorts, with the ice chest and a straw tote bag that held sun block and any number of other necessities only a woman would think of bringing, while Kyle took Dylan to the shore.

They found a perfect spot on a mound of grass near the water's edge. Hopefully the bass would be biting, but even if they didn't catch a thing, nothing beat a day of fishing.

Being near the lake brought back a ton of memories. Good memories of the many times he and Jimmy Hoben had kicked back and cast their lines into the fishing hole.

After baiting their hooks and casting out lines, Dylan and Kyle waited. And they talked—not about anything in particular, just the regular guy things, like why girls didn't like worms and whether the Wildcats would win another national basketball championship.

After a while, Dylan asked, "How come Milla would rather read a book than fish?"

"Who knows?" Kyle glanced over his shoulder and watched her lounging comfortably on the old yellow blanket, book lifted to block the sun. "Maybe she doesn't know how much fun it is to land a bass."

"Probably 'cause she's a girl."

"Some girls and ladies like to fish," Kyle said.

Dylan seemed to ponder that for a while, then said, "Maybe, but most of them don't like the same kind of things we do."

"Someday you're going to appreciate the differences between males and females," Kyle said, with a grin. "It can be frustrating at times, but a real pleasure, too."

"Maybe girls get better when they grow up," Dylan said. "My mom is pretty cool."

That was the truth. Kyle glanced over his shoulder again and spotted Milla's furrowed brow, her mind obviously in her book.

Enough of that, Kyle reprimanded himself. Then, trying to steer the conversation to the troubles the boy was having, he said, "Your mom says you go to summer camp."

"Yeah. At my school."

"Is it fun?"

"Sometimes."

"But not always?" Kyle asked, looking for that opening.

"There's this kid at camp," Dylan said, scrunching his freckled nose. "His name is Kirk, and he's really dumb."

Kyle knew Dylan's assessment of the boy had nothing to do with IQ. "What's so dumb about him?"

"He picks on kids and says really dumb stuff."

Kyle checked his line, then glanced off into the horizon. "What kind of dumb stuff?"

"You know. Like picking on a kid about things that don't matter."

Kyle didn't need to hear the details to know that Dylan had been bullied. "What's he been saying to you?"

"Stuff about my dad. You know."

Yeah, unfortunately, Kyle did know, and probably better than anyone.

"Listen, Dylan. The world is full of dumb people who make comments that hurt others. But you can't let them get to you."

"That's what my mom says." The boy shifted his weight and blew out a sigh. "I try not to, but sometimes it's hard."

"When I was your age, I had to deal with kids like Kirk, too."

"You did?"

Oh, man. Did Kyle need to go into the past? Dig up those old bones that he'd buried? Something in the boy's eyes told him he did. "I had to fight my way out of a lot of scraps, all because my dad didn't marry my mom."

"Did you get in trouble, too?"

Kyle blew out a sigh. "Yep. Got my nose bloodied more times than I can count. And spent hours in detention. Folks thought I was just a bad kid, but it was more than that."

"What do you mean?" Dylan asked.

"You and I have more in common than just getting in fights and getting suspended from camp or school."

"We do?" Dylan asked, his voice raising an octave.

"Did anyone ever tell you my dad's name?"

Dylan shook his head.

"Billy Bingham," Kyle said. "You ever hear of him?"

Dylan's eyes widened. "Billy Bingham was my dad."

Kyle shot the boy an easy grin. "Mine, too. Looks like we're brothers."

Dylan sat up and leaned forward. "No way. I got a brother?"

The kid had more half siblings than he knew, but Kyle kept that to himself. "Yep. I'm your brother."

"Wow, wait till Kirk the Jerk finds out about this." Dylan busted out in laughter. "Kirk has a big brother who's twelve. And he's an even bigger jerk. But you could kick his butt, no problem."

Kyle couldn't help the grin that broke forth on his face. "Slow down, buddy. I'm afraid my butt-kicking days are over."

Dylan's face dropped. "But having someone like you stick up for me would really make them back off."

That's all Kyle needed. Another playground reputation. His name was probably still a legend at every school in Creekside, the community outside of Binghamton where he and his mom used to live.

Hoping Dylan would go for a more rational approach, Kyle said, "I've got a better idea. I'll help you learn how to overcome their comments without fighting."

"You got some kind of secret weapon for jerks?"

"No. But I've got a great weapon for kids that are going to grow up and be something great someday."

"You do?"

"The only reason guys like Kirk tease guys like us is to see us get angry. They're trying to get a reaction out of us. So there's only one surefire way of fighting back and winning."

"What's that?"

"You've got to ignore them, no matter what they say. No matter how bad it hurts. Even if you have to smile and walk away."

"My mom said I gotta ignore him, but it's too hard."

"She's right. When Kirk the Jerk can't get you to react, he'll get bored with the game and leave you alone. Why don't you try it for a couple of weeks and see what happens?''

"Did it work for you?" Dylan asked.

"Yep. Except I didn't have a brother to show me how it was done, so I learned the lesson late in life." Kyle slipped an arm around the boy's shoulder. "And I'll tell you what. You give me a call each evening, after you get home, and let me know how it's working."

"Thanks," Dylan said. "It's going to be way cool having a big brother like you."

Kyle wasn't a big-brother sort of guy. Shoot, he'd grown up as an only child, never knowing his half siblings or his cousins. It had been a lonely life, in a way. Maybe that's one reason he'd gotten into so many fights—not all of which had been about his daddy.

Like a gunslinger of the Wild West, Kyle had come to accept the fact that there was always someone waiting in the wings, hoping to be the one who laid tough-guy Kyle Bingham low.

But that didn't mean Kyle didn't have friends. Jimmy Hoben had been his best buddy. His death after the camping trip had been so tough on Kyle. They'd been like brothers, he supposed. And that's why the teen's loss had struck such a brutal blow.

Maybe being a big brother was like being a grown-up buddy. Kyle wasn't sure what he could offer Dylan, but he'd give it his best shot.

If he could help make Dylan's life easier than his own had been, it was worth the effort.

Birds chattered in the treetops, and children's voices rang out in play. A light breeze swept across the lake, filling the morning air with the sights and sounds of a perfect summer day.

Several times Milla glanced up from her suspense novel to check on Kyle and Dylan. She couldn't catch the words, but she could see the smiles, hear the chuckles. They seemed to be bonding, which was good. Dylan seemed to be having the time of his life.

Bringing Dylan to meet Kyle had been a great idea. Maybe all the little boy needed was a man to take him under his wing once in a while. To make him feel special. The good-looking doctor ought to be able to handle that.

"Hey!" Kyle called from the shoreline. "How do a couple of hardworking fishermen go about getting something to eat?"

"They ask for it," Milla said, dog-earing her page and closing the book.

She took the turkey sandwiches from the cooler, along with apple slices, crackers and cheese. In moments she had the picnic lunch spread on the blanket.

When Kyle and Dylan joined her, her heart teeter-tottered in a strange way. In a family sort of way.

Milla had missed having two parents, missed having outings like this. It was one of the reasons she'd been so brokenhearted after her dad had bailed out on them.

But then again, she realized, sorting through her memories, the man had never taken her or her mother on picnics. Nor had he gone to any school functions. Come to think of it, her dad had left their family long before he left their house.

She wasn't sure if that made his absence any less painful, but she wasn't going to ponder it.

"So," she said, turning her attention to her son. "How many fish have you caught?"

"None yet," Dylan said. "I think they're sleeping."

"Not to worry," Kyle told the boy. "We're going to catch a whole lot of them before we get home."

Milla lifted a brow. "How can you be so sure?"

He shot her a crooked grin and winked. "We may have to drive back to the grocery store and catch them there."

Dylan roared with laughter. "Yeah. We'll catch one of those lobsters in the tank, the ones with their claws all tied up."

"Then we'll try to hook a tub of crab salad from the seafood deli case," Kyle added.

Milla couldn't help but join in the silly laughter. She appreciated the man's efforts, more than he knew. And she admired him for reaching out to an unhappy child.

"Maybe we can do something else together," Kyle

said, "next time I have an off-duty weekend." He glanced at Milla, as though looking for an okay.

Her heart nearly fluttered out of her chest, but she realized he was making the effort for Dylan. Not her.

He was, after all, dating an attractive blond nurse. Or was he?

"What about Karla?" Milla hated herself for asking, for bringing up the other woman's name. "Is she willing to give you up again?"

"We're not seeing each other anymore," he said.

In part, Milla was pleased. But the fact that Kyle had moved on to the next in line only reinforced the fact that he didn't stick with any woman for very long.

"Come on, Mom. Please?" Dylan pleaded, eyes glistening. "Kyle's my big brother. You just gotta say yes."

How could she tell the boy no? Having a brother, no matter what his age, was a big deal to Dylan.

"Okay," Milla said, hoping her reluctance didn't show.

A male role model was just what Dylan needed— as long as Kyle didn't walk away and desert Dylan when a boy needed a man the most.

Chapter Eight

Dylan's enthusiastic rendition of the fishing trip brought on a flurry of questions at home.

And it was just as well. Milla needed to level with her mother—at least as far as Kyle's association with Dylan went.

And as for her own involvement? That would remain a secret for the time being.

As expected, Sharon hadn't been happy to learn that her daughter had introduced Dylan to Kyle. And after the boy went to bed, the dreaded discussion followed.

"What were you thinking?" her mother asked. "You know how I feel about the Binghams."

"Kyle is a wonderful man," Milla said. "A top-notch doctor who attended Harvard Medical School. That's an admirable feat, and something he accomplished without having a father around the house. I think he'll make a great role model for Dylan."

"Humph." Sharon crossed her arms and sank back into the olive-green vinyl recliner. "Billy put a ton of money in a trust fund for his firstborn. It's anyone's guess what would have become of your doctor friend if he'd been left high and dry, like Dylan."

"Come on, Mom. Billy Bingham's plane went down before Dylan was even born. Had he lived, he probably would have set something up for Dylan, too."

"Well, he didn't. And when Dylan was orphaned, he was left with nothing."

"He has us."

"Yes, thank goodness," Sharon said. "But his mother, bless her soul, passed on. Now Dylan is motherless, and it's all Billy Bingham's fault."

Milla blew out a weary sigh. "Aunt Connie had placenta previa, a complication of pregnancy. We've talked about this before. The placenta attached too close to the cervix. As labor began and the cervix dilated, the placenta separated, causing her to hemorrhage. The doctors couldn't stop her bleeding."

"I don't need another medical explanation," Sharon said. "My baby sister died when she was only twenty-one years old. If that no-good Billy Bingham hadn't seduced her, she would still be alive.''

Milla hadn't argued. What was the point? Her mom was still bitter over the loss of the younger sister she'd adored.

As far as Sharon was concerned, the Binghams had, one way or another, caused most of the troubles in her life. And there might be some truth to that.

The late Gerard Bingham had owned the coal mine where Sharon's dad, Slim Johnson, had worked. Health insurance hadn't been provided for the employees. And when Slim died in a mining accident, his family was left without a way to pay for the chronic health problems Connie'd had as a child.

Gerard had been a ruthless businessman, from what Milla understood. And Sharon Johnson wasn't the only one in the community to blame the Binghams— or at least Gerard and Billy—for their troubles.

After venting a while longer, Milla's mother said good-night and went to bed.

But it wasn't over.

The subject continued to arise, each time Dylan asked to use the phone to talk to his brother. Usually Kyle was unavailable. But Milla had to give him credit. He always returned the boy's call.

Yesterday, Kyle had asked to speak to Milla, which surprised her. It also left her weak-kneed and tongue-tied, until she realized he'd called to talk about Dylan.

''I've got some free time on Monday morning,''

he'd said. "Can you bring Dylan by my place? I can take him to camp when we're done."

"Sure." Milla had been a little disappointed that Kyle hadn't called looking for her, but it pleased her to know he'd taken an interest in her son.

She did manage to get someone to cover her shift at the clinic on Monday, though. Just in case.

After all, she did have to drive Dylan to Kyle's house. And if he asked her to go along with them?

Well, why not? It was heartwarming to see the two brothers become acquainted. Besides, she had a personal reason for wanting to get to know Kyle better. He was the father of her baby. What kind of man was he? What kind of father would he make?

Would he want to be a part of her child's life? Or would a baby threaten his freedom?

"I hope you know what you're doing," her mother had said, before Milla and Dylan left the house.

"You'll have to trust me, Mom. Kyle and Dylan have a lot in common. Having a male role model will do him a great deal of good."

Milla could only hope that her words held true, that Kyle wouldn't tire of the boy, and that he'd maintain some kind of relationship with Dylan, even after Kyle left Merlyn County for good.

When Dylan came bounding into the living room, he grinned from ear to ear. "Okay, I combed my hair and brushed my teeth. Can we go now?"

Sharon merely frowned, then turned and walked

toward the kitchen, her opinion still hovering in the air.

Milla now had another reason to hope Kyle would be more dependable than his father had been. Her mother would never tire of saying, "I told you so."

"All right, Dylan. Let's go." Milla opened the front door, then led the way to her car.

"Aunt Sharon was in one of those weird moods again," Dylan said, as he climbed into the back seat. "Isn't she happy about me going with Kyle?"

His comment came as a bit of a surprise, since Milla and her mother were careful not to discuss certain issues in front of him, particularly Bingham-related issues.

"Maybe she wasn't feeling well," was Milla's only response.

In no time at all, they headed out of town. As they turned down Bluebonnet Lane, Milla watched carefully for Kyle's sage-colored triplex. She spotted it right away, but the place looked different in the daylight.

The springtime green lawns had been freshly mowed and trimmed. And along the concrete walk, an array of flowers lined the way, bursting forth in shades of yellow, red, purple and pink. The colorful display gave the plain, sage and beige buildings character, something she hadn't noticed at night.

Of course, when she'd followed Kyle home, her thoughts hadn't been on the landscape or the architecture. She'd been more interested in the man who'd brought her here. The man who'd kissed her senseless, turned her bones to cartilage and promised to send her over the edge in a burst of pleasure.

And he'd done just that.

But dwelling on bittersweet memories wouldn't do Milla any good. There'd be no more mindless nights of passion for her. Not with a man who couldn't make a commitment to just one woman.

Milla stopped the car in front of the end unit and scanned the quiet neighborhood. It seemed that most of the residents had either gone about their Monday business or remained inside for a quiet morning.

A short, matronly woman with a floppy straw hat, dirt-stained pink gloves and a clipper, stood beside a row of rosebushes that separated Kyle's yard from the one next door. She straightened and, using a gloved hand to shield her eyes from the morning sun, watched as Milla opened the door and slid from the car. "Hello, there."

"Good morning," Milla replied. "We're here to see Kyle Bingham."

"He's inside." The older woman smiled warmly at Milla, but caught her breath when Dylan climbed from the car. "Oh, my goodness."

"What's the matter?" Milla asked.

"That child is the spitting image of..." She looked at Milla, eyes wide. "Well, I'll be. It's like looking back in time."

Before the conversation could go any further, Kyle stepped onto the porch, in all his Viking splendor. A Norseman who sported a gold watch and designer clothes straight out of *GQ*.

"I can see you've met," he said. "Mom, these are some friends of mine. Milla Johnson is one of the midwives from the clinic. And this is her son, Dylan."

"Her son?" Kyle's mother did a double take, checking out Kyle, then Dylan, noticing the resemblance, then checking them out again, much like someone sitting courtside at Wimbledon.

Good Lord. Did the woman think that Dylan was Kyle's son? That he and Milla had created a child?

Well, that wasn't so farfetched. He and Milla *had* created a little one. But it wasn't Dylan.

As though trying to rope in her surprise and remember her manners, Kyle's mother stepped forward, pulled off one of the gardening gloves she wore and extended a hand to Milla. "Pleased to meet you. I'm Sally Woots."

The introductions moved swiftly, as Kyle explained his relationship to Dylan.

The woman accepted the news with grace, warming to Dylan immediately.

"You both look like your daddy," Sally said, a big, wistful smile tugging at her lips. "He was a handsome man."

And apparently a charmer, Milla wanted to add. But she didn't.

Sally chuckled, then cast a conspiratorial smile at Milla. "Well, shoot, I guess I don't have to tell you how good-looking Billy was."

Milla blanched. For goodness' sake, Sally assumed that she and Billy...

But why not? Dylan had, after all, been introduced as Milla's son, so it had been a natural assumption. She glanced at Kyle, hoping he'd set the record straight.

When he didn't Milla said, "I haven't started the official paperwork yet, but will in the next few days. I'm adopting Dylan. His mother was my aunt."

"Well," Sally said, as though trying to regroup and get the conversation back on a topic better suited for Dylan. "I've got a cookie jar full of chocolate chip cookies. Why don't you boys go inside and get a couple handfuls?"

"Come on," Kyle said to Dylan. "No one makes cookies like my mom."

When they'd disappeared into the beige duplex to the right, Sally said, "I hope I didn't say anything wrong. I always have this way of babbling before I think."

"Don't worry about it. Dylan doesn't even remember his mom. She died right after he was born."

"How sad. I'm so sorry to hear that."

By the look in Sally's eye, Milla had no doubt of

her sincerity. In fact, she'd made another observation about Kyle's mom. The pretty, down-to-earth woman who'd borne one of Billy's children didn't seem to harbor any resentment toward the man. Quite the opposite, actually.

"I can't get over it." Sally slowly shook her head. "Your son looks so much like mine did as a little boy."

As Kyle and Dylan walked out carrying a handful of cookies, Milla studied the two brothers. She couldn't help wondering what her own baby would look like.

Would it have Kyle's Nordic good looks? His blond hair and bright-blue eyes?

"The gardeners come tomorrow," Kyle said. "What are you doing out here, Mom? Don't you have to work today?"

"I love spending time in the rose garden. And I thought I'd get some fresh flowers for the table." She turned to Milla. "I just got a new job as a sales clerk at Book Nook, but they didn't schedule me until this afternoon."

"If you weren't so stubborn about accepting my help, you wouldn't need to work." He handed Milla a cookie, and she took it.

Mmm. He was right. Moist, chewy, chocolaty and loaded with fresh pecans. It tasted better than any cookie she'd ever eaten.

"I like providing for myself," Sally said. "And my new job is perfect for a book lover like me."

"Well, I guess we'd better go, Mom. I'm taking Dylan over to the schoolyard in Creekside." He looked at Milla, the depth of his gaze catching her off balance. "Want to join us?"

She nearly choked on the cookie she'd bitten into, but nodded. "Sure. Sounds like fun."

"Then let's go."

As Milla followed Kyle to his car, she couldn't help reminding herself why she'd agreed to go along. She wanted to be sure the budding relationship between Kyle and Dylan stayed on track. And she enjoyed watching them relate to each other.

But she feared it was more than that.

Deep inside, she liked pretending they were a family. And that scared her, more than she cared to admit, because Kyle Bingham wasn't the kind to commit to one woman for the rest of his life.

And Milla wouldn't settle for anything less.

Kyle hadn't visited his old stomping ground in ages, but the school looked the same, for the most part. They'd replaced the old monkey bars with a lime-green-colored climbing structure and added a new handball court.

He and Milla walked side by side, while Dylan happily checked out every nook and cranny of the playground.

The summer sun and an easterly breeze had blessed them with a pleasant day. And, surprisingly enough, Kyle enjoyed a nostalgic regression to the lazy days of childhood.

He glanced at the bell tower he and Jimmy had climbed. Mr. Miller, the principal, had used a ladder to bring them down. The two boys hadn't minded the detention, because they'd been playground heroes for nearly a week.

Walking on the elementary campus brought some of his schoolyard memories to mind, but each time he glanced at Milla or caught a whiff of her scent— something crisp and citrusy today—he was drawn back to the present, back to adult pleasures and pastimes.

She wore a pale green sundress that slid past the gentle curve of her hips and down to the middle of her shapely calves. It took nerves of steel not to slip an arm around her, pull her near and brush a kiss across her lips.

Milla seemed to work some kind of magic on him. And if he had ever had the inclination to commit to one woman, it would be to someone like her.

But he didn't have any family-type yearnings. And he never had. His bachelor life suited him.

She flashed him a playful smile, and he was struck by the power of his arousal. Since when had he gone bonkers for such a wholesome woman?

Since Milla had first caught his eye.

She wandered over to the swings then kicked off her shoes, revealing toenails tinted with cherry-red polish. And as she walked across the sand, a smile crept onto her face. She fingered the chain that held a swing, then sat on the strap of the seat and dug her toes into the sand.

Unable to help himself, Kyle approached from behind. "Want me to give you a push?"

She glanced over her shoulder and shot him a youthful smile that slammed into his chest. "All right."

Kyle took hold of the chains that held her seat, pulled back, then released her. Each time she came within reach, he pushed her away. And she came flying back.

Her hair blew in the breeze, and she laughed, the lilt of her voice lingering in his ears.

What made him think being around Milla would lessen the attraction he felt? If anything, having her near only stirred his blood and heightened his arousal even more.

"I can go faster and higher than that," Dylan said, joining them at the swing set.

"Let's see you try," Milla called, pumping her legs to increase the momentum.

Kyle laughed. "You two are setting off the competitor in me. Watch out."

Then he joined them, swinging with wild abandon,

feeling like a kid again. Only better. Happier. More carefree.

Who would have guessed that taking a kid to the playground could be so pleasant, so darn enjoyable?

"Can you do this?" Dylan asked, before jumping from the swing and flying through the air. He landed on his feet, then turned in triumph.

"I can do it even better," Kyle said, letting loose, broad-jump style.

"How about you?" Dylan asked Milla. "Think you can beat us guys?"

She shot him a challenging grin, then seemed to sober. "Nah. I'd probably fall on my bottom and embarrass myself."

Or hurt the baby, Milla thought.

Caught up in the fun, she'd nearly taken the challenge. But that would have been a bad idea, especially if she'd taken a hard tumble on the sand.

The unplanned pregnancy might have come as a shock, and she might dread having a child out of wedlock and having to deal with the professional repercussions, but a flood of maternal love swept over her. She wanted to shield her baby from harm. Wanted to nurture it and protect it.

When the swing slowed to a stop, she joined Kyle and Dylan on the grass. "Okay, you guys. Now what?"

"How about a touch football game?" Dylan asked. "I brought my ball."

"All right," Milla said. "If we're choosing sides, I get first pick. And I'll take Dylan."

Kyle laughed. "Okay, you've got a deal."

The next thing Milla knew, they'd blocked off a playing field, using their shoes to indicate imaginary goal lines.

"Let's loosen up your arm," Kyle suggested.

Milla watched the football spiral down the field, watched Dylan laugh and whoop it up, having the time of his life. She didn't know when she'd seen him so happy. Or when she'd had such unbridled fun.

"Okay, I'm warmed up," Dylan said. "Let's start the game."

In a huddle of two, Dylan suggested a hand off, to surprise their single opponent.

Milla agreed, snatching the ball. And as Dylan hooted with delight, she ran barefoot across the grass toward the goal line marked by her two sandals.

Kyle chased after her, his long strides quickly catching up. He grabbed her by the hips and pulled her back. His musky scent was nearly overwhelming, and as she turned, she stepped on a sticker and yelped, losing her balance.

Oh, no. The baby, she thought, no longer concerned about the sharp prick to her instep. Kyle caught her in an attempt to hold her upright, but they both fell. He rolled, to take the brunt of the hit and soften her fall.

"Are you all right?" he asked.

"I think so." She lay on top of him, trying to catch her breath. But as her breasts splayed against his chest, as his musky scent blended with her orange-blossom fragrance, her hormones flared, her heart pounded and her blood pumped. A heated look passed between them.

For a moment she thought Kyle might be as caught up as she was.

Lordy, how that man stirred her juices. She had the urge to wrap her arms around his neck, pull his lips to hers and kiss him as if there was no tomorrow.

But there *was* a tomorrow.

And a lawsuit hanging over her head. A pregnancy yet to be revealed. A good chance that Kyle might walk out of her life the way his father had, abandoning so many countless other women who'd fallen for his charm.

Instead of following her desire, Milla rolled to the side and laughed off the arousing effects of being in Kyle's arms. But her heart continued to race, and not from physical exertion.

"Are you okay?" he asked.

"I'm fine," she lied.

Sure, physically she was all right. No blood, no bruises. No aches or pains. But on the inside?

Something weird was going on. And she didn't know what it was.

It was just infatuation, her conscience told her— nothing more, nothing less.

But that seemed like an inept attempt to mask the truth.

Milla feared she was coming close to falling in love with her baby's father, if she hadn't done so already. The possibility scared the dickens out of her, especially since the object of her affection wasn't likely to make any kind of commitment to her or the baby.

Kyle placed a hand on her shoulder. "Are you sure you're all right?"

"Absolutely. I'm tougher than I look." She tried to conjure a smile that would hide her lie.

He smiled, accepting her explanation, it seemed. But he wasn't that gullible.

The threat of abandonment hovered around her, and Kyle hadn't yet left her side.

Chapter Nine

Three days after the touch football game had become a bit too heated for comfort, Milla wasn't even close to shaking Kyle Bingham from her mind.

Or from her heart.

Determined to ignore the jumbled emotions that pestered her during the quiet times, she threw herself into her work. She took on extra home health-care shifts, a division of the midwifery clinic that allowed qualified nurses to visit new mothers at their homes.

On Thursday afternoon, as Mari Bingham had requested, Milla met with Lillith Cunningham, the PR director of the hospital who would play a role in the preparations for the trial.

Mari had hired the PR whiz from New York City,

hoping Lily would be able to smooth the edges of the protest over the development of the new research facility, as well as the bad press that was sure to come from the lawsuit.

Milla hoped so, too. With each hour that passed, with each day that the Canfields' malpractice suit forged ahead, the stress piled on. And although she realized there was no magic formula, no waving of a wand to solve her dilemma, Milla hoped the attractive and stylishly dressed PR director would have something to offer her, some proposal that would fix things.

From what Milla understood, Lily Cunningham had done extensive fund-raising and promotional work for VIP clients in New York. So she ought to know her stuff.

"How have you been holding up, Milla?" Lily asked, as they sat across from each other in the director's office.

"All right, I suppose. The whole mess is pretty unsettling, especially since the charge is so unfair." Milla tucked a strand of hair behind her ear. "I'm not sure whether anyone has told you, but Kyle Bingham has agreed to testify in my defense. He's prepared to tell the court that the Canfields didn't take proper care of the umbilicus."

"I realize you didn't do anything wrong," Lily said. "And the court will probably decide in your favor, assuming the lawsuit makes it that far. But the media attention alone will put the clinic—and you—in a bad light.''

''Is there anything we can do to counteract that?''

''As the hospital spokesperson, I'll control the press coverage to an extent.''

''Can I do anything to help?'' Milla asked, feeling frustrated as well as powerless.

''For one thing, you'll need to keep your comments to a minimum, especially when cornered by the press. A standard 'no comment' is probably best.'' The stylish blonde in her early forties sat back in her chair. ''In the next couple days I'll come up with some mock questions that you can answer truthfully. Then we'll practice the wording for use during a deposition. Or the trial, if things go that far.''

Milla nodded, but before Lily could continue, Milla's pager went off. She glanced at the lighted display and recognized the telephone number. It was Sue Ellen Henderson, a young woman expecting her third baby.

Sue Ellen was already five days overdue. And since she'd only experienced four hours of labor with her last child, Milla had instructed her to call at the very first sign of contractions.

Milla blew out a soft sigh and looked at the PR director. ''I'm sorry, Lily. Can we reschedule this meeting? I'm going to need to respond to this page.''

''Of course. It will give me time to develop those questions. How about tomorrow afternoon? Around this same time?''

"That's fine with me." Milla stood, then extended a hand to the attractive blonde. "Thank you. I appreciate your help."

"I'll see you tomorrow."

Milla headed for the nurses' station, where she placed a call to her patient. "Hi, Sue Ellen. It's Milla."

"You told me to let you know as soon as labor started, and I'm pretty sure it has."

Milla didn't doubt the woman's instincts, but she wanted more information. "What makes you think you're in labor?"

"Well, I've had a nagging backache all morning. I'm having some contractions. They aren't exactly painful, but they're uncomfortable and seem to be coming about ten minutes apart—more or less. I've also been spotting a little bit, and I think my water is leaking."

"I'll be right there," Milla told the expectant mother. "It shouldn't take me longer than fifteen minutes."

Milla hung up the phone, eager to be on her way. But before she could go to the locker room for her purse and gather the supplies she would need, Mari Bingham approached. "Got a minute?"

"Just barely. I've been called to a home delivery."

Mari nodded. "I'll make it brief. I received the results on the drug sample I sent to the lab."

"And?" Milla asked.

"It wasn't Orcadol."

Milla's stomach knotted, and she voiced the un-spoken words that hovered around them. "Someone has been stealing the Orcadol and replacing it with another painkiller."

Mari nodded. "That's what it looks like."

"I still haven't noticed anything unusual," Milla said. "And I've been watching."

"Since it appears to be an inside job, it won't be obvious."

The thought that someone they worked with—a doctor, nurse or midwife—had been stealing drugs sickened Milla. She struggled to come up with some words of wisdom or support, but couldn't think of anything to say. The news was shocking, and the ram-ifications left her speechless.

"We can talk about this later, since you need to go," Mari said.

Milla glanced at her watch. She *did* need to leave. Sue Ellen's pregnancy had been uneventful, and the baby had dropped into position. There didn't seem to be any reason why things wouldn't progress quickly.

"Go to your delivery," Mari said. "I'll talk to you later." Then she continued on her way, carrying a burden she didn't deserve.

But there was no time to ponder the injustice. And no time to dawdle. Milla's first obligation was to her patient, so she hurried to get her things, then left the clinic.

As she stepped out the main door and into the af-ternoon sunlight, she paused. Oh, good grief. In her haste and concern, she'd nearly forgotten about Dylan. He needed a ride home from day camp this afternoon.

Her mother wasn't doing much driving these days. The accident that had injured her back and neck had also left her nervous and fearful when traveling on the city streets. And even if Sharon had no qualms about driving, she and Milla had only one car.

Sometimes Milla asked one of their neighbors to pick up Dylan. And just last week her mom had needed a ride to the doctor. The neighbors had all been gracious, but Milla hated to become a nuisance.

One other option came to mind.

Did she dare ask Kyle to step in? He was, after all, Dylan's brother. And he'd taken a liking to the boy. Was it too much to ask?

Maybe not.

Besides, it would give Milla a chance to see how the man would react to taking on a familylike responsibility, especially since she needed to tell him about the baby soon.

Maybe he'd take the news better than she'd anticipated.

Kyle studied the X-ray of one of his last patients of the day, a twelve-year-old girl who'd fractured her wrist while riding a bike. She'd knocked a growth plate out of whack, and he was going to call in an orthopedic surgeon.

His shift was nearly over, having started before five

o'clock that morning, and he was looking forward to going home, kicking off his shoes and watching a ball game on his big-screen TV.

He made his way to the front desk, where one of the E.R. clerks sat, answering the telephone and handling admissions.

"Dr. Bingham," the dark-haired woman said. "Milla Johnson called. She left her number."

"Thanks." Kyle took the note bearing Milla's name and cell phone number, yet kept his mind on his task. "Marlis, can you get a hold of Brad Kemp with Mountain View Orthopedics? I'd like him to look at the Peterson girl."

"Certainly."

Kyle fingered the note and wondered why Milla had called. She'd been pretty quiet after they'd taken Dylan to the school playground on Monday. After they'd landed on top of each other.

Had she sensed his reaction to holding her again, to being close enough to savor the scent of her body lotion, to stroking her back, to feeling her flush against him?

She must have, because she'd sure pulled away fast.

Had his arousal been that evident? Had it scared her off?

Probably. It had sure made *him* uneasy to realize how badly he'd missed holding her. How damn badly he wanted to get her back into his bed and stoke the fire that burned inside her. He wanted to bury himself in her softness and hear her cry out in release, just as his own climax burst free.

She'd seemed to withdraw, but that hadn't bothered him. He needed to distance himself, too. He'd needed to sort through things and figure out what to do about the blasted desire that raged inside of him.

Maybe that's why he'd steered clear of her for the past few days. He knew women like Milla usually wanted more than a man like him was willing to give.

Kyle wasn't into forever type commitments. And he wasn't even sure he could offer her a two-year plan until his residency was over. It wasn't his style. And he sure as hell wasn't about to promise something he couldn't fulfill.

Taking a break from each other gave them both a chance to let the dust settle. To come up with some kind of solution or compromise.

He hadn't come up with anything, though. Because the urge to sleep with her again was too strong and *not* making love with her wasn't an option.

For that reason he'd contemplated calling her, but decided to give her another day or so to think about things, to change her mind about renewing a sexual relationship with him.

And now she'd called him, which was good. Better, actually.

Or was it?

There was only one way to find out. He picked up the phone and returned her call.

She answered on the first ring.

"It's Kyle. What's up?"

"I, uh…" Her words seemed to stall. Was she having second thoughts about contacting him?

"I'm on my way to a home delivery," she said. "And I just realized Dylan is stuck at summer camp. I'm sure you're probably too busy, but is there any chance you could pick him up at the school and take him home for me?"

Kyle glanced at the clock on the wall—two-twenty-five. "Sure, I can get him, but not for another hour or so."

"That would be fine," she said. "You can drop him off at my house, if you don't want to be stuck with him."

Stuck with Dylan? For some reason Kyle didn't feel stuck at all. In fact, he really liked the kid.

And Dylan liked him, too.

Sometimes the boy's smile was full of hero worship, which seemed a bit misplaced, since Kyle wasn't a hero in any way, shape or form. But Dylan's admiration had touched him just the same, making him want to set a good example and be the kind of guy who deserved the boy's respect.

"I don't mind at all," Kyle told Milla. "Go on to your delivery and don't worry. I'll keep Dylan until you get finished."

"Are you sure it's no bother?"

"Not at all." Kyle looked forward to spending time with his little brother.

He'd also like to see Milla again—later tonight, when she came for the boy.

Maybe then, when she stood before him—on his turf—he could figure out how their last unavoidable embrace had affected her.

Was she having as much trouble forgetting as he was?

He hoped so.

Getting her back into his bed would be much easier that way.

An hour later Kyle arrived at Daniel Boone Elementary and wandered back to the playground, where Milla had said Dylan would be.

"Kyle!" Dylan shrieked, making no secret of his pleasure at being picked up by his big brother. "Are you taking me home?"

"To my place," Kyle said.

"Cool!" Then Dylan turned to the director of the kids' camp. "Mr. Rick this is my brother, Kyle. He's an adult."

Apparently the fact that Kyle had graduated from med school wasn't nearly as impressive as his age. Or maybe Dylan didn't care about anything more than having a brother to call his own.

After Kyle greeted Mr. Rick, who'd apparently already been alerted to his arrival instead of Milla's, Dylan led Kyle over to the handball courts and introduced him to a redheaded boy named Kirk.

So this chubby, freckle-faced kid was the notorious Kirk the Jerk.

The heavyset boy seemed to momentarily cower when he looked up, making it obvious that Dylan had already told the kids that Kyle was a butt-kicking tough guy who didn't cotton to anyone messing with his little brother.

Kyle supposed he should talk to Dylan about that in the car, reminding him that adults—particularly pediatricians—didn't go around fighting playground bullies.

But Kyle probably would have done the same thing, when he was Dylan's age, so he really couldn't blame him. It would have been great to bring in a ringer, to have someone in his corner to cover his back.

Kyle might have sported a black eye, a skinned knee or a bloody nose like a badge of courage, but his injuries had hurt. And he'd oftentimes had to fight like hell to keep the tears at bay and maintain a bad-ass attitude.

As several boys edged forward, curiosity on their faces, Kyle extended a hand to Kirk. "It's nice to meet a friend of Dylan's."

The boy scrunched his face as though unsure of what to do, then he reluctantly shook Kyle's hand.

"Do you boys like ice cream?" Kyle asked the kids who'd gathered around.

Dumbfounded, the boys glanced at each other as though it might be a trick question.

Kirk was the first to nod. "Yeah, we like ice cream. Why?"

"Because I thought Dylan and I could pick up some ice-cream bars this evening and, if it's okay with Mr. Rick, we could bring them to summer camp tomorrow and share."

"Cool," a dark-haired boy said.

Kyle didn't see the act as a bribe, but rather as an olive branch, which seemed like a far more viable plan than a good butt kicking.

And if the ice cream didn't work?

Well, he'd have to figure out something else.

After talking to the director and getting an okay for the afternoon snack, Kyle signed Dylan out, then led him to where he'd left the car.

"Are you hungry?" he asked on their way to the parking lot.

"Yeah. I'm always hungry in the afternoon. Are you?"

"I'm starving."

Five minutes later Kyle drove Dylan through Binghamton until they reached South Junction Burgers, a mom-and-pop restaurant that served juicy hamburgers, hand-cut fries and the thickest milk shakes east of the Mississippi.

The old building used to be located on South Junction, but during a thunderstorm a few years ago, it was struck by lightning. The proprietors decided to reopen at this downtown location, but didn't change the name—probably because they wanted to bring their reputation with them.

"I came here once before," Dylan said.

"Only once? Don't you and your mom like burgers?"

"We love 'em. But it's kind of expensive, going to restaurants and stuff. So we don't go out unless it's a treat, like a birthday or something."

Kyle didn't like the idea of either Dylan or Milla being on such a tight budget that they could go out to eat only once or twice a year. But he supposed that's what life would have been like for him, had his father not provided a generous child support check each month. And then there was that hefty trust fund for his college education and his future.

Dylan, he realized, hadn't been as lucky.

Funny, but this was the first time Kyle had actually looked at his childhood and found something to be happy about, other than having a mother who loved him to the point of spoiling him rotten.

Once inside the restaurant, they chose a corner booth and studied the menu.

"What are you going to have?" Kyle asked Dylan.

"A hamburger, but I don't want mayonnaise or onions or mustard. What are you having?"

"Something bad for my arteries," Kyle said with a smile. He was usually pretty good about staying away from greasy food, but this was a special outing. At least, it felt like one. "I'm going to have a double bacon cheeseburger and an extra-large order of fries.''

''After we eat, are we going to the store to buy the ice cream for the kids at camp?'' Dylan asked.

''I suppose so.'' Kyle got to thinking about what Mr. Rick had said. They'd need sixty-two ice-cream bars. And he wasn't sure if he had that kind of room in his freezer. He could bum some space from his mom, but, knowing her, she probably had her entire refrigerator packed from top to bottom.

Of course, he'd also have to deliver the ice cream to camp tomorrow. Or ask someone else to do it.

He flipped over the menu, checking out the desserts. And when the waitress came by to take their food order, he asked, ''What are the chances of me buying about sixty-five ice-cream sundaes and having them delivered to Daniel Boone Elementary School tomorrow afternoon?''

''Well,'' the auburn-haired waitress said. ''Let me check with the manager. What time would you need them?''

''After the lunch rush and before your dinner crowd comes in.''

She nodded, wrote down the burger and fry orders, then disappeared. Moments later she returned, bearing a smile. ''The manager said there'd be no problem making those ice-cream sundaes. We can even deliver them for you, but there'll be an extra charge.''

''No problem. Let me know what I owe you.''

A few minutes later the waitress brought their

chocolate milk shakes and handed Kyle a bill for the ice-cream order. He looked it over, then whipped out his credit card. "Put it on this."

"You got it," she said with a smile, then left him and Dylan to enjoy their shakes.

"Thanks, Kyle."

For the ice-cream sundaes? It was no big deal. He could afford it.

"You're the best big brother a kid ever had."

Well, Kyle wasn't sure that was true. What did he know about being a brother? Not much. He'd never had that big-happy-family experience.

Maybe that's why a wife and kids had never been in his game plan. But as Dylan's praise warmed his heart like a flood of hot-fudge sauce drizzled over a brownie à la mode, he was glad he'd decided to give the big-brother thing a try.

He slid the boy an easy smile. "You're a pretty cool brother, too."

The waitress brought their meals, and they continued to chat while munching on burgers and chomping down fries.

"Have you been ignoring Kirk, like I suggested?" Kyle asked.

"Yeah. Kind of. I haven't been getting in trouble as much, either."

"Why do you get in trouble?"

Dylan dipped a fry into a puddle of ketchup on his plate, popped it into his mouth, then shrugged his shoulders. "I don't know. 'Cause I want the kids to think I'm cool."

"I used to like to get attention, too," Kyle said, realizing just how much he and Dylan had in common. "But it made things tough on my mom. Now that I'm older, I wish I'd understood how badly she felt each time she was called into the principal's office because of me."

"I didn't think about that." Dylan frowned. "I don't want my mom to feel bad or get in trouble with the principal, just 'cause of me."

"That's a good attitude to have." Kyle hoped his words might make things easier for Milla. She had a rough row to hoe as a single mom, just as his own mother had.

As a pleasant afternoon unfolded into early evening, Kyle and his little brother drew closer. Having the boy around was kind of nice. And if Kyle hadn't been so eager to see Milla for another, more personal reason, he would have called her and asked if Dylan could spend the night.

Hopefully, her delivery was going well and there wouldn't be any complications to keep her away until morning.

Kyle was looking forward to seeing her later tonight—more than he cared to admit.

Chapter Ten

Milla arrived at the Henderson place, a three-bedroom house in a quiet neighborhood. It was the kind of home she hoped to have someday, with a big shade tree in the front yard and a swing set and playhouse in the back.

Tom Henderson, a maintenance man at the Merlyn County Courthouse and Administration complex, opened the door. "Oh, it's you. Good! Come on in."

"How's she doing?" Milla asked.

"Great, but I'm sure glad you're here." Tom led Milla through the cozy little house that had been decorated in a country style, with colors of light green, beige and lavender. Bowls of potpourri and candles provided the scent of lilac throughout the rooms.

Sue Ellen sat in an overstuffed easy chair, rubbing her stomach and using a focused breathing technique during what appeared to be a strong contraction. Rather than distract the laboring woman, Milla washed up before greeting her.

Within fifteen minutes of her arrival, Milla had examined Sue Ellen in the bedroom and assessed her progress. "Your labor is moving right along. And your contractions are strong. We should have a baby before long."

While Tom prepared dinner for the two children, Sue Ellen felt the need to bear down. And after Milla determined that Sue Ellen was fully dilated, she was given the okay to push. The baby came quickly, and at 6:07 p.m., a red-faced baby boy slid into Milla's hands. He immediately burst into a rebel yell, alerting his father and siblings of his arrival.

"Is he all right?" Sue Ellen asked.

"Absolutely beautiful." Milla placed him on his mother's stomach, while she cut the cord and noted he'd scored a 9 on the Apgar scale.

Sue Ellen nursed her son right away, and the baby quickly settled in, latching on to the breast.

One day soon, Milla would hold her own newborn baby. She'd feel her milk let down and watch her infant son or daughter nurse.

Milla glanced at Tom and saw the look of wonder on his face. Would Kyle be there with her? Did his growing relationship with Dylan mean he had a paternal side he hadn't recognized?

"Look at that little guy," Tom Henderson said. "He's sure got my appetite."

Sue Ellen laughed. "And your long legs."

"Mine aren't quite that skinny," the tall, lanky man said with a chuckle. "But with the way he's chowing down, he'll fill out in no time at all."

"Can I look at him?" Christy, a six-year-old pixie with long blond pigtails asked. "Please?"

"Me, too." The younger girl edged closer, a look of awe on her little face. "He's the cutest little baby in the whole world."

"I don't know about that," their father said. "You two were pretty darn cute, with those big blue peepers and little bald heads."

"Wanna see pictures of us?" Christy asked Milla.

Milla smiled. "I'd love to."

"I'll go get our baby books," the little girl said, as she dashed off, her four-year-old sister on her heels.

Milla relished the closeness of this family and the love that overflowed. And she was glad to be part of their new baby's birth.

If anything, the warm fuzzy feeling that settled around her heart made her realize the time had come to tell Kyle about the baby. About *their* baby.

Maybe she'd tell him tonight.

Just seven hours after walking into the Henderson's three-bedroom house, Milla was able to pack up her things and leave.

"If you have any questions or concerns, please give me a call."

Sue Ellen, who sat propped against the headboard in the couple's four-poster antique bed, flashed Milla a Madonna-like smile. "I'm sure we'll be just fine. Thank you for helping me have our baby at home."

"It was my pleasure," Milla said. "I wish all the babies I delivered had such loving families."

Then she left the Hendersons to enjoy their newest blessing, her thoughts on the precious babe growing inside her.

About a quarter after ten, Milla arrived at Kyle's house, tired, but still riding on the emotional rush that came after witnessing the miracle of birth.

As she walked to the front porch, she caught the faint scent of night-blooming jasmine in the air. Funny, she hadn't noticed the fragrance before, on the night she'd followed Kyle home. Maybe she'd been too nervous, too focused on what was about to happen.

She felt some of that same nervousness now, although she didn't know why. In spite of her attraction to the handsome bachelor, romance wasn't an option.

Not if she wanted to protect her heart.

And certainly not until she saw his reaction to the news of their baby.

Milla rapped lightly on the door and after waiting only a moment, Kyle let her in.

"Dylan crashed about an hour ago," he said, indicating the child stretched out on the sofa.

An awkwardness settled around her—the shy, enamored adolescent kind. "Thank you for taking care of him for me."

"No problem."

Milla couldn't keep her gaze from lingering on the man standing before her, looking as sexy as a dream come true in a pair of faded jeans and a white T-shirt.

Usually dressed to perfection, the casual wear and uncombed hair gave him a rebellious look she found incredibly appealing. And difficult to ignore.

As though he'd read her mind, he slid her a half-cocked smile that sent her nerves zipping and zapping, her pulse racing, and her senses reeling.

"Come on in." He stepped out of the way, allowing her into the living room.

She hadn't been inside his house since the night they'd made love, and the return visit brought back a flood of memories, as well as a heavy shot of desire.

Hoping to ignore thoughts of lovemaking, she scanned the room, spotting Dylan's shoes and dirt-stained socks on the floor and two empty bowls on the coffee table, next to a deck of cards.

"I sure appreciate you helping me out like this," she said.

"I'm not always free, but it worked out fine today."

"He really likes you." Milla nodded toward Dylan. "I'm sure this was a real treat for him."

Kyle studied the boy sprawled on the sofa and smiled. "I like him, too. He's a good kid, and we had a great time."

She was glad to hear that. "Not having a man around the house has been tough for him."

"I'm sure it has been." Kyle shrugged. "I grew up without a father in the house, without a male role model. I wasn't sure what I could offer him."

"You've given him something I can't give him." She took a breath, deciding to test the waters. "You'll make a great father someday."

Kyle chuffed. "I have no intention of being a dad. I'm not cut out to be a family man. Being a big brother is about as close as I want to get."

Milla nearly blurted out the truth, nearly told him that was too bad. That he was going to be a father whether he liked the idea or not. But with Dylan lying on the sofa, so innocent and unaware, she decided to wait.

What would one more day hurt? It wasn't as though she intended to keep the baby a secret from him. Besides, she was barely four weeks pregnant.

Hoping to shrug off her heavy thoughts and wanting to give her hands something to do, she picked up the bowls that appeared to have held strawberry ice cream. "I'll take these to the kitchen for you."

Kyle followed her to the sink, the musky scent of his mountain-fresh aftershave taunting her, reminding her of things best forgotten.

Hadn't he told her that he had no intention of being a father?

Then, for goodness' sake, why couldn't she shake the attraction she felt for a man who wouldn't step up to the plate?

Because Kyle Bingham held some kind of hold on her, that's why. Or maybe because she hoped that, given time, he'd actually get used to the idea of being a father. Or of being a husband.

She turned on the spigot and allowed the water to fill both bowls. It seemed a mundane task when what she really wanted was to face him. To allow her common sense to fly by the wayside. To wrap her arms around his neck and kiss him for all she was worth. To yield to temptation one last time, before their brief relationship blew up in her face.

But instead of letting herself ask for a repeat of the night they'd touched the moon and stars, she stood firm, continuing to rinse the bowls long after the last hint of pink had gone down the drain.

"Can we talk, Milla?"

"Talk about what?" Her voice waffled, and she hoped he hadn't noticed.

"About you and me."

His gaze snagged hers, and even though sexual awareness nearly knocked her for a loop, she still knew that getting involved with him wasn't a good idea.

The problem was that while her mind had no trouble believing it her body wasn't listening.

She turned her head toward the stainless-steel sink, trying to break eye contact with the man who aroused everything but her common sense. "Nothing has changed."

But that couldn't be further from the truth. Things had changed, big-time. Kyle just didn't know it yet.

And her hormones must be doing a real number on her, because she actually felt sorry for him. Sorry for his loss. Hers, too, she supposed, because the thought of not ever kissing him again nearly tore her in two.

Kyle reached from behind her and shut off the faucet. Then he took her shoulder and turned her around. To face him. To face what they'd done. What they felt.

"You're wrong, honey. Things have changed whether either of us wants to admit it or not." Then he lifted her chin and placed his mouth on hers.

The kiss deepened into a raging desire that left her breathless yet aching for more. She twined her wet fingers in his hair, drawing his mouth closer to hers, his tongue deeper.

She should turn her head, push him away. But her brain shut down, and her body took over. Unable to help herself, she leaned into him, into his erection. A moan formed low in his throat, and a feeling of feminine power soared through her.

He wanted her. Badly. And, heaven help her, she wanted him. Wanted this. Even if it was the last time she'd ever be in his arms.

She had the sudden urge to feel him, flesh to flesh,

to feel him inside of her, filling the ache of emptiness. His hands slid under her blouse, stroking her skin, sending a heated shiver to her core.

"I've missed touching you," he said, as he tore his mouth from hers to nibble her neck.

She'd missed it, too. The heat. The way their bodies seemed to fit as though made only for each other.

They stood in the kitchen, panting, breathless. Ready. But Milla couldn't allow herself to succumb to the sweet assault. Not tonight. And maybe not ever.

What had gotten into her? Dylan was sleeping in the other room.

With more regret than she thought possible, she placed both hands on his chest and, breaking the embrace, pushed him away. "We can't let that happen. Not here and not now."

"I have a lock on my bedroom door," Kyle said, brushing a strand of hair from her face. His fingers left a blaze of heat where they'd touched.

"No. It's not a good idea. I'm sorry. I lost my head."

"Why isn't it a good idea?" Kyle asked. "We've got something special."

"Because of the lawsuit," she said, although her mother's anti-Bingham sentiments rang in her ears.

"That's not a good enough reason," Kyle said. "No one needs to know we're seeing each other on a personal level."

He was right. The real reason she didn't want to make love with him again was because she feared letting herself go, feared falling deeper in love with a man who wouldn't stick around after the last firework sputtered and died.

Kyle's ardor, which was so apparent here and now, would probably cool the minute he found out about her pregnancy.

And he would find out. In the next day or so. And she suspected he would turn his back on her and their illegitimate child, just like his dad had done so many times. Just as her own father had done.

Kyle would probably agree to pay child support, but a child's emotional needs were just as important as its physical ones.

And so were a woman's.

"What's the real reason you keep pulling away from me?" Kyle asked. "I know you want me as badly as I want you."

"That's not true," she said, her voice faltering. She wanted him more. And she was the one who stood to lose her heart and soul to the man.

So why not tell him the truth?

The time might not be right to tell him about the baby, but she could be honest, level with him about her fears.

"I won't make love with you again unless there's a commitment between us," she said, "a commitment that will last. Can you give that to me?"

Milla's words slammed into Kyle, nearly knocking the wind out of him. It would be so easy to lie, to tell her what she wanted to hear. But he'd always been truthful with the women he dated, even if it hurt them.

A commitment? She was asking too much.

He felt something powerful for Milla. But was it enough? He'd never felt an urge to stick with one woman and he had no reason to believe anything had changed.

The thought of making a promise like that now—a promise he didn't know if he could keep—smacked him like a cold, wet towel in a locker room free-for-all.

''I'm not sure that I can give you the kind of commitment you want,'' he said. ''The kind of commitment you deserve.''

''That's the real issue here, Kyle. I might be able to escape with my heart intact, if I walk away now. But if I allow myself to get involved any deeper with you…''

Her words trailed off, but the meaning didn't. Milla cared for him, enough to fear a broken heart.

And that scared the liver out of him, for more reasons than one.

Sure the fear of commitment slapped him hard. But so did this incredible urge to protect her, to keep her from hurting.

And hurting Milla wasn't something he wanted to do, not when he had no plans of staying in Binghamton after his residency. If he cared about her, he needed to back off. To stop pushing for more.

She ran a hand through the silky strands of her hair.

"Listen, Kyle. I need to take Dylan home. And you're right. We do need to talk. But I'm not up for it tonight."

He nodded, although he figured they'd said all that needed to be said. She'd made herself pretty damn clear.

And even though her words—and her leaving— were unsettling, he couldn't ask her to reconsider or to stay.

He *wouldn't* ask her.

"Let me carry Dylan for you," he said, wanting to shake his feeling of helplessness.

He scooped his little brother into his arms and carried him out to Milla's car. After settling the sleepy boy in back and buckling the seat belt, he made his way to the driver's door. "You made your point. I'm not sure there's any reason to talk about this tomorrow. But if you want to, I will."

"There were a few things left unsaid," she told him. Then she turned the ignition and started the car. "I didn't mean to put a damper on the evening."

But she had.

A number of ladies had asked Kyle for a commitment, and he'd always graciously refused. Letting them go had never bothered him. But this was different.

Maybe it had been hard to let go of the sex. Hadn't it been the best he'd ever had?

Kyle sure hoped that was the reason, because a heaviness in his chest left him feeling awkward.

Unbalanced.

Alone.

''Thanks again for picking up Dylan,'' she said. Then she stepped on the gas and drove away.

Kyle stood on the porch, until her taillights disappeared. And even after she'd gone, he continued to stare into the darkness.

Chapter Eleven

Milla hadn't slept worth a darn last night. Thoughts of Kyle had kept her awake, heated memories torturing her with what might have been.

She'd relived each touch and kiss, but she'd also relived the words that had passed between them in his kitchen.

I won't make love with you again unless there's a commitment between us, a commitment that will last. Can you give that to me?

I'm not sure that I can give you the kind of commitment you want, he'd said.

She knew that wasn't what he meant. The real message rang loud and clear in his frozen expression, in his possum-in-the-headlights gaze.

Kyle hadn't indicated having any feelings for her, other than desire. So there was no reason for her to believe that he loved her. Or that he would ever love her. And although she'd never expected him to, the reality still hurt—far more than she'd imagined.

By the time the sunlight peered through the bent slats in the miniblinds, Milla gave up all hope of sleep.

"You don't look rested," her mother said, when Milla climbed from bed.

"I'll be okay."

"Your eyes are red and puffy, honey. Maybe you should call in sick."

A simple solution—and appealing—but impossible.

"I have a home visitation scheduled first thing this morning." Milla grabbed a pair of black slacks and a white blouse from the closet. "But if I can, I'll try to come home early."

"I'm worried about you."

Milla wasn't up for a heart-to-heart with her mom this morning. "I'm fine."

"You flip-flopped last night like a beached flounder," her mother said. "Is something bothering you?"

"I was just thinking about the future," Milla said, hoping the generic but truthful statement would suffice. "You don't need to worry about me." Then she left the bedroom, wandered into the bathroom and locked the door.

Standing in the small, windowless room, she studied her bone-weary image in the mirror. Straggly hair. Pale complexion. Puffy circles under bloodshot eyes.

Her mother was right. She looked like heck. And as much as she wanted to blame Kyle, she couldn't. She'd known he was a dyed-in-the-wool bachelor going into this…this what? Star-crossed relationship? Brief sexual fling?

Either way, she'd known the outcome from day one.

But Milla was glad she'd told him the truth; glad she'd spilled her guts and her heart. She *did* have a lot to lose, if she agreed to be his lover again. And in spite of the gaping hole in her heart, there was a freedom in her soul.

As the old adage said, the truth had set her free—free of temptation, since Kyle wouldn't be pursuing her any longer.

But one last item of business still weighed heavy on her mind—the child they'd created.

Maybe she should have told him about the baby last night, but it hadn't seemed like the time to throw everything at him. First things first, she supposed.

The baby issue was best left to a new day, a new conversation. After all, her pregnancy didn't have anything to do with her reluctance to get involved with Kyle. It merely complicated things.

After taking a long, lukewarm shower intended to make her bright-eyed and bushy-tailed, Milla dabbed a bit of her mother's pancake makeup under her eyes to cover the puffy, dark circles. Then she brewed a strong pot of coffee and drank two cups, hoping a double dose of caffeine would see her through the day.

Neither effort seemed to help much, she realized, as she hustled Dylan out the front door and into the car.

Milla didn't have anything pressing to do today, other than the home visitation scheduled for this morning. Maybe she could take the afternoon off and catch up on the sleep she'd lost.

"I can't wait to get to camp," Dylan said. "We're going to play with water balloons on the upper field. And Kyle is having ice-cream sundaes brought to us."

"Good," Milla told him. Ever since Kyle had taken an interest in him, Dylan's attitude had changed.

She left the happy boy with his friends at school, then drove out to the home of Claudia Montgomery, a young, single mother who was recuperating from a C-section she'd had a week ago. Claudia lived outside of town, in a secluded, rural area, off an old county road.

Unlike the neighborhood in which the Hendersons lived, Claudia's house was isolated and surrounded by a scraggly copse of trees. Milla supposed some people preferred not having neighbors, but she wouldn't like living so far out in the sticks.

As she made her way up the front walk, she heard a baby cry. Good. That meant Claudia was awake.

Milla knocked at the front door. When no one answered, she tried the bell, just in case the woman hadn't heard her knock, which was certainly possible with the infant screaming like that.

Still no answer.

Maybe Claudia was in the shower.

Milla continued to wait patiently on the stoop.

And the baby continued to cry.

"Claudia?" Milla called. "Are you there?"

No answer, except for the infant's wails. In fact, the baby's voice sounded hoarse. Did it also sound weak?

Her heart rate accelerated, as she banged on the door. "Claudia! Open up."

Still no answer.

Oh, dear God. Was something wrong? Milla tried to turn the knob, but found the door locked.

Don't jump to conclusions, she told herself. Everything was probably fine. Most likely Claudia was in the shower and couldn't hear the baby or the bell or the knocks. And, no doubt, she was moving slowly because of her surgery.

Still, a cold sweat gathered at her brow, and her pulse began to pound in her ears. Something was wrong.

Milla made her way around the house, walking through grass in desperate need of a lawn mower and past a garden overrun with weeds. She tried to open the sliding door in back. Locked.

Next she went from window to window, but couldn't find one to budge. Did she dare grab a rock and break the glass?

What other choice did she have? She had to get inside, had to check on the mother and child who lived here alone.

She blew out a ragged sigh, then spotted a way in—a bathroom window at the side of the house that was open a crack. If she could find something to stand on, she might be able to get inside. Milla scanned the yard and saw a weathered lawn chair. Hoping the wobbly thing didn't collapse, she stepped up, slid the window open, then climbed into the dark, musty house.

She followed the baby's cry down the hall.

"Claudia?" she called. The strength of her voice belied the butterflies in her tummy. "It's Milla Johnson with the Foster Clinic."

When she opened the bedroom door, she gasped. "Oh, my God."

The young mother lay on the bed, her eyes wide open, her face ashen. Pills that looked like Orcadol dotted the baby-blue bedspread.

An overdose?

Milla felt for the carotid artery in the base of Claudia's neck, finding the skin stone-cold and no sign of a heartbeat. Unable to do anything for the mother, she reached into the bassinet and lifted the infant.

"It's all right," she whispered. "I've got you, little one."

She fumbled for the phone while trying to comfort the baby and dialed 911. "This is Milla Johnson, a midwife with the Foster Clinic. I've come to the house of one of our patients, Claudia Montgomery, and found her dead. I think it's a drug overdose."

"We'll send the sheriff," the man on the line said. "And the coroner. Have you got an address?"

"It's about five miles out on the county road. Take a left at Cottontail Lane, which is a dirt road. There's a mailbox at her drive, with 1379 painted in black."

When Milla hung up, she looked at the newborn, noticed the mottled complexion, the way the baby boy drew up his legs and cried in pain.

Claudia had been breast-feeding. And if she had overdosed on painkillers, she may have transferred the drugs to the baby.

Milla reached for the phone to call 911 again, then thought better of it. By the time the ambulance got way out here, it could be too late.

She looked at the infant, at the little tufts of black hair and a dimple on the chin. "I promise to do my best to help you, little guy."

With nothing but the newborn's safety on her mind, she grabbed a sample of the pills on the bed, snatched an infant carrier from the floor in the bedroom, placed the child in it and rushed to her car.

She could drive to the hospital faster than waiting for the ambulance.

* * *

Twenty minutes later Milla arrived at the E.R. entrance and lay on her horn. By the time she'd gotten the baby out of the car, a nurse and an orderly rushed outside.

"I have a possible drug overdose," she said. "Get the pediatrician on call."

"That's Dr. Bingham," the orderly said. "I'll go get him."

Thank goodness, Milla thought, clutching the baby tight and following the nurse inside. Kyle would know what to do.

Milla glanced down at the tiny infant and whispered a prayer. She wasn't sure why, but she felt an emotional attachment to the baby boy who struggled for life.

Maybe it was the rescue and the realization that he might have died if Milla hadn't arrived. Or maybe it was a surge of hormones that had jump-started her maternal instincts into action. Either way, she wasn't going to leave the baby's side.

Kyle arrived, just as the newborn was placed on an exam table. "What have we got?"

"A six-day-old infant, seven pounds at birth, full term. The mother died of an apparent drug overdose." Milla pulled out the pills she'd recovered from Claudia's bedroom and showed them to Kyle. "I'm not sure what this is, but it might be Orcadol."

Kyle nodded, yet kept working over the baby.

"The mother was breast-feeding," she added, "so

there's a possibility that we have a case of transference.''

Kyle didn't respond, although Milla knew he'd heard and kept her comments in mind while assessing the baby.

Professionalism had kicked in, and anything that had gone on between them in the past weeks or the words they'd spoken the night before no longer mattered. The only concern in this small corner of the E.R. was the tiny baby who fought for his life—a six-day-old boy who'd lost his mother.

Milla thought about Claudia's next of kin. She supposed that was a matter for the sheriff to decide. And then a sudden realization dawned. Claudia had been referred to the midwifery program at the clinic by her sister—Darlene Canfield.

The malpractice charge hovered over her, like a dark, ominous shadow, and her heart sank to the pit of her stomach.

Surely Milla wouldn't be blamed for doing something wrong this time. She'd saved the newborn's life.

Or had she arrived too late?

Fear clutched at her chest, as she looked at the baby being poked and prodded. The emotional bond grew steadily. But now his fate had become even more personal.

She couldn't let this baby die. And if that meant fighting beside Kyle all day long, that's what she'd have to do.

Without waiting for a lab tech to arrive, Kyle drew

blood from the infant. And while he did so, Milla slipped from the room to call Mari Bingham. The director needed to know Milla's suspicion, that Orcadol might be involved.

After she'd placed the call and asked Mari to have someone cover for her, she returned to Kyle's side, determined to do whatever she could to help.

At four o'clock Milla called her mother and asked if she could possibly get one of the neighbors to pick up Dylan from camp.

"Yes, I'm sure I can," her mother said. "But I thought you were going to try and get off work early so you could rest."

"I'm fine," Milla said, ignoring her mother's concern. Then she rushed back to the NICU.

Back to the baby.

Back to the dedicated pediatrician's side.

Together Kyle and Milla worked through the evening to stabilize the critically ill newborn.

Finally, when it appeared their efforts had succeeded, Kyle slid her a weary but appreciative grin. "You're quite a trooper, Milla. You must be beat."

"I didn't sleep well last night…" She paused, realizing what she had implied. But it had been the truth. And she no longer wanted their relationship— or rather their conversations—to be muddled by dishonesty. "Anyway, I'm doing all right. I must be running on adrenaline."

"You didn't need to stay and help me. But I'm glad you did. You're one hell of a nurse, as well as a midwife.'' His gaze seemed to caress her hair, her face, then lingered on her eyes, drawing her into some inner place that revealed his sincerity.

She might not have his love, but she'd earned his respect. "Thanks."

He glanced at his gold watch, then looked up and smiled. "How about a bite to eat? The cafeteria won't close for another twenty minutes."

She was hungry, even though she hadn't allowed herself to think of anything but the critically ill newborn since this morning. "Things are probably picked over, but even a wilted salad and a dried-out sandwich sound pretty good right now."

"Come on." He lifted his hand as though to touch her back and guide her through the door, but gestured to the exit instead.

Had he intended to reach for her, then changed his mind? Or had she merely tried to make something out of nothing?

They continued down the hall side by side but without touching. Still Milla felt an invisible bond between them, a connection that had been missing in the past.

It seemed as though they'd reached some kind of understanding. Some kind of solid ground on which they could work.

Then again, maybe Milla was too darn rheumy to trust her instincts, particularly when it came to Kyle.

It was late; she was exhausted.

And there was too much on her heart and mind.

* * *

While making their way to the cafeteria, Kyle had felt an incredible urge to slip an arm around Milla, to pull her close. And not just because of that damned attraction that continued to plague him. There was something else at play, something other than sex.

Maybe it was the same kind of feeling that followed two teammates into the locker room after winning a championship in a game that had gone into overtime.

Hell, Kyle didn't know what it was, just that he and Milla had made a valiant effort today. And it had paid off. God willing, the baby boy would live.

They stood before an empty lettuce bowl and veggie-littered salad bar. There wasn't much to choose from at this late hour, so they'd decided to share the last ham sandwich and have a couple of bowls of minestrone soup.

Other than the guy who ran the cash register, Kyle and Milla were the only ones in the eatery. Still, he led her to a small table in a far corner of the room, wanting privacy.

As they ate, Kyle studied the woman across from him. The clip that once held her hair up now listed to the side. And several tendrils had escaped. Whatever makeup or lipstick she'd worn had faded away. Still, Kyle doubted he'd ever seen a more attractive woman.

Milla had an aura of beauty around her that was hard to ignore. And impossible to forget.

"I know you plan to go into research." She picked up a napkin and blotted her lips. "And you'll probably do wonders. But I've got to tell you, Kyle. You've got a knack for medicine. And I'd sure hate to see you give up working with patients."

He shrugged, unsure of what to say or how to respond. He'd been planning to go into research for so long that he'd never considered anything else.

"For what it's worth," she said, "I marveled at your skill with that baby today."

"Thanks. You did a pretty admirable job, too. Want to give up midwifery and become an E.R. nurse?"

"No, I love what I do."

He smiled. "So then you probably understand how I feel. I'm not ready to give up my dream to do research."

"Like I said, I'm sure you'll do a great job."

"Thanks."

They ate in silence for a while, yet Kyle was very much aware of the woman across from him—aware of the light sprinkle of freckles across her nose, aware of the dimples on her cheek when she smiled. Aware of her orange-blossom scent.

But it was more than her femininity drawing him.

Kyle had always respected Milla as a medical professional, but more so now that he'd worked closely with her. And he admired her for adopting Dylan, too.

No, there was much more to Milla Johnson than met the eye. And he liked what he saw.

Interestingly enough, it didn't seem to matter whether she was dressed in a classic black dress and sitting across a candlelit table or wearing a white lab coat with a fluorescent light flickering on a Formica tabletop.

Admiration for the lady lingered, like the faint citrus scent that taunted him.

He wanted to take her hand and give it a squeeze. But he knew better than to touch her. He had too much respect for her, for her feelings.

And knowing that he had the power to break her heart made him uneasy. He wouldn't want to hurt Milla for the world. In fact, he had this goofy need to protect her. But he'd never been one to don a superhero cape. It wasn't his style.

"Kyle," she said, the soft sound of her voice settling over him, stirring his senses. "Did you know the baby we saved is related to the Canfields?"

"No, I didn't." He saw the worry on her face, the concern.

"I hope they…" Her words trailed off, but not their meaning, not her fear.

"You saved that child's life, Milla. And if anyone is to blame for this, it's his mother."

"I know."

Again Kyle wanted to reach out, to offer her something more than words. But quite frankly, he was afraid to allow his emotions to surface.

They let the subject of her concern drop, but he

knew she was still worried. And there didn't seem to be a damn thing he could do to help.

When they finished eating, Kyle walked her out to her car. The soles of their shoes crunched along the pavement, and the lonely sound of a hoot owl called out from somewhere in the night.

Kyle had the urge to say something, to do something—like kiss her goodbye.

But Milla had made herself clear. She cared too much about him, and for him to pursue any kind of relationship might hurt her in the long run. No, he wouldn't kiss her. He respected her too damn much to play with her feelings—her feelings for *him*.

The fact that she might even love him a little ought to make him want to duck for cover. Instead, it felt kind of nice.

But Kyle was still hell-bent on remaining a foot-loose bachelor. He tried to conjure that old love-'em-and-leave-'em attitude, tried to rekindle that hot-blooded urge to enjoy whatever lady he was with—until the next one came along.

He glanced at the pretty brunette at his side and felt a surge of desire. He wanted to kiss her again. Right now. But he didn't think he could take her in his arms and leave it at that, so he kept his hands to himself.

"Good night," he told her. "Drive carefully."

"I will." She slid him a dimpled smile that touched his heart, then got into her car and started the engine.

But instead of standing in the parking lot and watching her go, he headed for his BMW.

In the past he'd had a happy-go-lucky feeling when a woman left. But now he felt a strange sense of loneliness.

Instead of dwelling on it, he kicked up his pace and climbed behind the wheel of his car.

He had to get home before the lonely night swallowed him alive.

Chapter Twelve

Too exhausted to fret or worry, Milla crashed the moment her head hit the yellow-checkered pillowcase in her small, cramped bedroom, and she didn't wake until noon.

When she finally wandered into the living room, she found her mother sitting on the sofa that had been given new life with a floral slipcover. As usual, her mom had the drapes pulled to keep out the bright morning sun.

Milla ran a hand through the tangled strands of her hair. "I can't believe I slept this late. Thank goodness Mari told me to take the morning off."

"I'm glad you finally got some rest, honey." Her mom took a sip of something in a cup—probably herbal tea, which was the drink she favored. "I was worried about you."

Milla scanned the small, dark-paneled room. "Where's Dylan?"

"I tried to keep him quiet after he woke up, but ever since Dr. Bingham bought that ice cream for his friends, Dylan's been jabbering a mile a minute about the fun he's having at camp and chomping at the bit to go back and play."

Kyle had certainly come up with a great idea. The ice cream had worked like a charm. Too bad Milla hadn't thought about doing something like that earlier. Of course, she couldn't have afforded to buy sundaes for the group, but she could have made cookies or cupcakes.

"So where *is* Dylan? He's never this quiet."

Sharon smiled. "I had a good night's sleep, too. And since I didn't have to take any pain medication, I drove him to camp."

That didn't happen very often, and Milla was glad that her mother had swallowed her anxiety and driven the car. "Thanks, Mom. I know how hard it is for you to get behind the wheel."

"Well, I probably ought to rustle up my courage more often. I don't want to feel cooped up for the rest of my life."

Milla plopped down in the green vinyl recliner across from the sofa and decided to broach a subject they needed to discuss—well, one of them, anyway. "I know you're not too keen on me adopting Dylan, but I'd like to talk about my reasons for wanting to make things legal.''

"It came as a surprise, that's all." Sharon took another sip, then placed her cup on the saucer that rested on the end table. "It's not that I don't want you to adopt him. I just don't see the need. You're a very big part of his life. In fact, you always have been."

That was true. Her mother had been so devastated when Connie died that Milla had taken over most of Dylan's care and had been the first to bond with him.

"I know things are okay the way they are, but Dylan wants to have a mother to call his own. I'd like to honor his need for a real mom. And to tell you the truth, I'd love to call him my son."

Sharon took a deep breath, then slowly let it out. "I wish my sister were here. She should be the one raising her child, not you or me."

As much as Milla hated to go into the usual Billy-Bingham-is-an-SOB routine, she allowed the conversation to follow a natural course for a good reason. She had a few questions she'd never actually voiced—in part because she'd always avoided any comment that might make her mother launch into an emotional tirade. And also because the issue had never really affected her before.

But now she hoped broaching the subject might help her prepare for her upcoming talk with Kyle. "How did Billy react when Aunt Connie told him she was pregnant?''

"Connie never got a chance to tell him. Billy had just bought a brand-new plane and took a notion to fly to New Orleans so he could play in some high-falutin' poker game on a fancy riverboat. And even though every other pilot in the county had sense enough to stay on dry ground, that cocky fool thought he was a real hotshot."

"So he took off when it wasn't safe?" Milla asked.

"Everyone knew how bad the weather was going to be, but Billy thought he could beat the coming storm. And he was dead wrong."

The gambler had taken a chance and lost, Milla realized. But she went back to the original question she'd asked, the answer she'd been waiting for.

Milla had always assumed that Billy had turned his back on her pregnant aunt, or at least, that's what her mother had always implied. But Billy hadn't known that Aunt Connie was pregnant.

So, if he never knew about Dylan, it didn't seem as though he should be blamed for not doing the right thing.

The man was thirty-six years old when his plane crashed—too young to die. But by that time, twenty years had passed since the first of his children had been born. He might have matured, and maybe he would have been ready to settle down.

And there was another possibility, Milla realized. Aunt Connie might have meant more to him than the other women.

For some reason, Milla needed to cling to the hope

that the man would have done the right thing, eventually. "If Billy had known about the baby, he might have married Aunt Connie."

Sharon clicked her tongue and shook her head. "For goodness' sake, Milla. Look at the man's track record. He wasn't the marrying kind."

And neither was his firstborn son.

But just how much did the two men have in common? They were both too darn handsome for their own good, and women seemed to gravitate toward them like hungry bear cubs to a sticky chunk of honeycomb.

But Kyle wasn't a gambler like Billy had been. At least, Milla hadn't seen anything to suggest that. Not yet, anyway.

So what kind of man was the father of her unborn child?

Her heart wanted to sing his praises. But her mind wasn't so sure. How would Kyle react when Milla told him about the baby?

Would he get angry? Or would he merely withdraw emotionally, leaving Milla to raise the child alone, as a single mother?

But even if Kyle refused to be a loving husband, he might prove to be a supportive father. Look how good he was with Dylan. Of course, as a grown-up brother who lived out of the house, he was free to call the shots and determine just how involved he wanted to be.

Well, there was no use speculating. Milla would find the answer to all of those questions soon enough.

Milla stopped by the NICU to check on the Montgomery baby before her shift at the clinic began. His color was much better than when she'd left him last night.

"He seems to be improving," a woman's voice said from behind.

Milla turned to see Karla, the pretty blond nurse Kyle had once dated, the woman who'd stood happily at the handsome doctor's side.

Karla offered a warm smile, but Milla was struck by an awkward sense of jealousy.

"I'm glad he's doing better," Milla said. "A child shouldn't have to be born addicted to painkillers."

Karla edged closer to the isolette, closer to Milla. "I heard you and Dr. Bingham worked on this little guy all day yesterday."

"Yes. It was touch-and-go for a while."

Karla smiled. "Everyone is talking about your efforts. You two worked very well together."

Was Karla digging for information? Trying to find out whether Milla was the new woman in Kyle's life? Or was she merely making conversation and trying to be nice?

"I'm not so sure that we did anything monumental. We just didn't give up. Kyle's a great doctor, and it was an honor to work beside him."

"He's also easy on the eyes," Karla said. "Don't you think?"

Milla nodded. "Yes, I suppose he is."

"I'd kind of hoped things would click between us." Karla shrugged and sent Milla a wistful smile. "But I sure crashed and burned."

"What do you mean?" Milla asked, unable to still the curiosity. Or the hope that Kyle and Karla hadn't slept together. It really wasn't her business, and she had no right to care, she supposed.

But she did.

In fact, a very childish, selfish part of her wished the man would be cursed with celibacy for the rest of his life.

Yeah, right. Fat chance of that.

Milla wasn't proud of her jealous streak or the urge to become territorial with a man who would never be hers, but that didn't seem to matter. And she couldn't help the way she felt.

"Well, I didn't make any secret of my intentions," Karla continued, "but he wasn't interested. And other than polite chitchat or professional conversations, he's never mentioned going out or doing anything with me since."

"Dr. Bingham isn't the only goldfish in the pond," Milla said, hoping to take her own trite response to heart.

Karla shrugged again. "If he weren't such a big catch and *way* out of my league, I'd really have my feelings hurt."

Milla opened her mouth but couldn't think of anything appropriate to say. Unlike Karla, she hadn't crashed and burned, but she wished she had.

Now wait a minute. That wasn't really true.

Hadn't she made up her mind to be honest about her feelings for Kyle?

As much as she wanted to believe that making love to Kyle had been a big mistake, she couldn't bring herself to admit the lie. Their night of lovemaking had been too special, too memorable.

And speaking of memories, in less than eight months she would have a little flesh-and-blood reminder that would last her a lifetime.

"By the way," Karla said. "Are you going to the hospital picnic? It's this Saturday."

The picnic. Milla had nearly forgotten about it. Every July, the hospital and the clinic put on a huge party for the families of the staff. They held it at The Rec, which was what the locals called the Gerald Bingham Recreational Facility.

The board hired a catering company that brought in an old-fashioned chuck wagon and barbecued on the spot. The food was always great, and everyone had fun, especially the kids.

"Yes, my son and I are going," Milla said. "How about you?"

"I wouldn't miss it for the world. Besides, I'm on the planning committee this year." Karla smiled. "Your little boy is really going to have a good time. We're having the usual activities, like the three-legged race and the watermelon-eating contest. But we've got some neat relays and some new games planned.''

"Sounds like fun.''

"I'm sure it will be.'' Karla glanced at her watch. "Uh-oh. We've got a shift change coming up, so I'd better get busy.''

Milla had to go, too, but before she managed a step, a woman's voice sounded from the entrance of the NICU.

"Excuse me. Can you tell us where we can find Claudia Montgomery's baby?''

Milla turned to see Darlene Canfield and her husband standing before her. Her heart rate accelerated, as her nervous system kicked into play, demanding a fight-or-flight reaction—but her body couldn't seem to decide which would benefit her the most.

Before she could respond, Kyle strode into the NICU and spoke directly to the Canfields. "Can I help you?''

Milla wanted to throw her arms around him and thank him for taking charge and for taking the heat.

"We're looking for our nephew,'' Darlene said. "We were told he was here.''

"This is the baby.'' Kyle nodded toward the isolette where Milla stood.

Joe Canfield pointed at Milla and frowned. "What's she doing here?''

Kyle wanted to flatten the guy, right on the spot.

Instead, he held his temper. "Would you please step out into the hall?"

Joe looked at his wife, then seemed to take note of the other three critically ill infants in the unit. "Okay. Come on, Darlene."

"You, too," Kyle said to Milla.

She shot him a look that said, "Why me?" but followed them out the door and into the hospital corridor.

"Let's get something straight," Kyle said. "Milla Johnson is one of the finest nurses and midwives I've ever had the privilege to work with. And if it hadn't been for her, the Montgomery baby would have died."

"What do you mean?" Joe asked.

"She went to a scheduled home visit and found Ms. Montgomery dead from an overdose. Her son was critically ill, because of the drugs his mother had taken. And he was also severely dehydrated."

"Yeah, well we appreciate that," Joe began.

Before the jerk could interject a but Kyle continued. "To tell you the truth, I didn't know until late last night whether the baby would live or die. And even though your nephew wasn't Ms. Johnson's patient, she stayed and worked along with me to save the baby's life."

"She's just trying to make up for nearly killing our daughter," Joe said.

"That's ridiculous. I was the physician on call when you brought your baby in to the E.R. The primary cause of her infection was the bandage you applied to her umbilicus, keeping it moist and unable to dry out.''

"We didn't bandage her little belly button until it became red," Darlene said.

"I saw the size of those disposable diapers she was wearing. Were you using those?"

"Yes," Darlene said. "They were given to us as a shower gift, and we decided to use them before purchasing the little newborn size."

"Did you fold them down, to prevent them from rubbing against the umbilicus?" Kyle asked.

"Should we have?"

"Shut up, Darlene. He's trying to blame us."

"I'm not blaming anyone," Kyle said. "But neither should you."

Darlene wiped a tear from her eye. "We just love her so much, and when she got so sick..."

"How's your daughter doing?" Kyle asked.

"Just fine." Darlene sniffled. "Isn't she, Joe?"

"Yeah. She's growing like a weed, now that she's on formula. I told Darlene her breast milk wasn't any good. You should have seen it, Doc. Looked clear and kind of blue—just like nonfat milk."

"That's what breast milk is supposed to look like," Kyle said. "But I'm glad the formula is working out for you."

"I love giving her a bottle," Darlene said. "And now I can tell how much she's getting."

Kyle always advocated breast-feeding, except in

cases where the mother was uncomfortable nursing. Some new mothers tended not to offer the breast often enough, which is what he thought had happened with Mrs. Canfield.

"I didn't mention it before," Kyle said, "but your daughter wasn't getting enough milk, and her immune system was probably compromised. The oversize diaper irritated the umbilicus, and when it reddened, you covered it with a gauze bandage in an effort to do the right thing."

"It wasn't because of the way she cut the cord?" Joe asked, nodding toward Milla as though she were a stump in the pasture.

"Absolutely not." Kyle placed a hand on Darlene's shoulder. "I'm glad your daughter is growing and doing well. You must be doing a great job."

Darlene smiled, then glanced at her husband. "Under the circumstances, maybe we should drop that lawsuit, honey. Our daughter is doing fine. And if Dr. Bingham says it wasn't Milla's fault…"

Joe made a gruntlike sound, then shrugged. "We'll talk about it when we get home, Darlene. But I guess we ought to be thankful everything worked out okay."

Kyle glanced at Milla and saw the sense of relief in her eyes. But he also saw signs of sympathy.

Milla approached the woman who'd accused her of malpractice. "I'm sorry about your sister, Darlene."

The tears slipped down the young mother's eyes. "Me, too. Claudia was always a wild little thing. But

I thought once she got pregnant, she'd quit messing around with drugs. I guess I was wrong.''

"You came to see her son," Kyle said, reminding them of their first objective. "Who will take care of him?''

"We aim to,'' Joe said. "We'll raise him like he was our own little boy.''

Kyle nodded, then said, "Go on in and see him. If you'll give me a few minutes, I'll come in and discuss the treatment and talk about when you might take him home.''

As the Canfields entered the NICU, Kyle looked at Milla, saw the gratitude in her eyes, the appreciation on her pretty face.

"Thank you,'' she said.

For what? Being honest? And doing his job? He didn't deserve her adoration—or the sappy feeling it evoked in him. "I figure that once the Canfields have a little time to think things through, they'll see reason. I'm hoping this mess won't have to go to court.''

"Me, too.'' Then she did something that surprised him. And just about knocked him to his knees. She gave him a hug that nearly sent him over the edge.

Her scent, something light and breezy and laced with wildflowers, accosted him, making him want more. More of her scent, more of her touch.

As her breasts splayed across his chest, their bodies fit together in a complementary way—soft and hard, gentle and strong.

Normally Kyle didn't care for public displays of

affection. Yet as they stood in the hospital corridor, he wanted to pull her close, nuzzle his face into her neck. Lift her mouth to his.

No doubt, she'd meant the embrace to be warm and sincere, yet Kyle wanted to take it to another level, make it a prelude to heavy breathing and hot sex.

She dropped her arms, stepped back, then blessed him with a smile that made his heart go topsy-turvy, as if she thought he was some kind of masked avenger.

Instead of making him balk or deny her silent accolades, he wanted to pound on his chest, Tarzan-style, and let out a primal call of the wild. Her son—his little brother—was starting to make him feel the same way.

And speaking of the boy…

"Do you and Dylan want to go with me to the picnic on Saturday? I thought he and I could be a team for some of those games and races."

They'd had a father-son event at Kyle's school once, where the dads enjoyed a field day with their kids. Kyle had gotten in one of his biggest fights later that afternoon, with the braggart who'd won first prize. When his mom had questioned him about yet another black eye, he'd shrugged off the competition and the fight.

"It was no big deal," he'd told his mother, which was the same thing he'd told the principal before his mom arrived.

But it had been a big deal and something he'd

never forgotten. As an adult, looking back, he realized the day would have gone much smoother if he'd had a man to round out his team.

"Sure, we can go with you," Milla said. "Although, we probably should meet you there."

"Because of your mom?" His chest tightened, and he felt himself tense. Would he ever step out of his father's shadow? Would he ever make peace with the Bingham blood that flowed in his veins? Probably not. That damn cloud would probably plague him the rest of his life. "Is your mother still blaming me for being Billy Bingham's son?"

"Actually, Mom likes the changes she's seen in Dylan since you've entered the picture. I'm hoping she'll be able to put aside her bitterness and get on with her life." She offered him a dimpled smile. "It's your call whether you want us to ride with you or not."

Did he want to go together—with Milla and Dylan?

Actually, he did, even though the idea made him feel like a family. And that was odd.

He'd never placed much value on that kind of thing before. Maybe because he'd never really felt as if he had a family, other than his mom.

The mother-son thing was easy to do. And so was being a brother. But Kyle was pretty leery of the rest of it. Being a husband or father wasn't the kind of lifelong job he wanted to take on. Too much responsibility, he supposed. Responsibility that would tie him down.

Milla glanced at her watch. "I really have to get going. I'd only meant to come check on the baby before I started work. I'm going to be late. Why don't you call me, after you decide."

"I'd like to go together," he said, as though afraid the option would be taken away the moment she turned her back. "If you don't mind."

"That's fine." Then she flashed him a smile, before taking off down the hall at a brisk pace.

He stood there for a while, watching her go, which seemed to be a habit he'd gotten into lately. Yet, a sense of family settled around him.

Milla, Dylan and him.

It was an odd sensation, an unusual thing to contemplate. A scary thing, actually.

Milla had asked for a commitment, which might be okay. He sure hoped that she didn't mean marriage, which would have sent him running off with his tail between his legs. The thought of matrimony had always scared the hell out of him.

If Kyle gave Milla what she wanted—a commitment—would something come of that? Something lasting?

On her part maybe. But on his?

He wasn't sure.

But assuming he had some big, life-altering change of heart and actually contemplated marriage, what then?

Would Milla consider marrying a man like Kyle? A man without a legitimate claim to family ties?

It all came back to the Binghams, didn't it? Back to him not measuring up. Not being good enough.

He supposed that that underlying fear had spawned each of his fights as a kid. And as an adult it contributed to his don't-fence-me-in attitude with women.

Deep inside, Kyle was scared to death of falling head over heels, just like a sap. Then finding out the woman he loved wanted more out of life than a Bingham wanna-be.

That's why he kept women at a distance.

And why he would continue to do so.

Chapter Thirteen

On the day of the hospital picnic, Kyle parked in front of Milla's house. But before he could get out of the car, Dylan raced outside, slamming the screen door behind him.

"You're here!" the boy yelled as he skidded to a stop. "My mom is almost dressed. But I was smart. I've been ready since last night, because I slept in my clothes."

Kyle laughed, tugging gently on the bill of Dylan's blue baseball cap. The hat covered his head and probably hid the fact that he'd combed his hair the night before, too, and didn't see the need to waste time doing it again this morning. Kyle noted the rumpled red T-shirt and the bright-eyed smile.

But what the heck. Picnics were supposed to be fun.

"Have you got on a pair of running shoes?" Kyle asked. "We're going to have to be pretty fast if we want to win a prize in that three-legged race."

Dylan stuck out a foot with laces dangling and smiled. "I got these new shoes all broke-in at camp. And I'm one of the fastest kids in the whole third grade. I even beat some of the fourth-graders, too. You and me are gonna win every single race."

The screen door swung open, and Milla walked out wearing a pair of white shorts, a bright yellow, scoop-necked T-shirt and a pair of legs that belonged on a Broadway stage. Legs that had once wrapped around him, drawing him deep inside her.

Kyle just stood there, gawking at her like a hormone-laden adolescent.

She tossed him a pretty smile, then looked at Dylan and scrunched her face. "That shirt must have been shoved in the bottom of your drawer. It's all wrinkled. Why don't you go in and change?"

"He looks fine," Kyle said, winking at the eager little boy. "Come on. Let's go."

Ten minutes later they arrived at The Rec, a huge recreation facility the legitimate branch of the family built in honor of Gerard Bingham. And whether the folks in Merlyn County cared about Gerard's contributions to the town or not, the community had a great place to congregate and play.

The grounds and complex provided an Olympic-size swimming pool, both indoor and outdoor basketball courts, football and baseball fields with bleachers and four lighted tennis courts.

Inside the massive building were rooms for aerobics, table tennis and air hockey. The Rec also provided space to host community meetings and events.

Built on donated land, the complex sat along the winding mountain road that led to the Bingham estate—a place Kyle had never been.

A place he no longer cared to visit.

Kyle supposed he should be proud of the Bingham Foundation, but the generosity they'd shown nameless strangers didn't impress him. He still bore the scars of their refusal to acknowledge him.

"Your family has done a lot for the city," Milla said, as she scanned the grounds.

"I may carry my dad's name, but bloodlines don't make a family." The response was a little more blunt and curt than Kyle would have liked, and he wished he could reel in the words and soften the tone.

Okay, so he still carried some of that bitterness he'd had as a kid. He could have sworn he'd shrugged it off years ago.

Milla didn't respond, and when he glanced across the seat, she wore a somber expression.

He wasn't sure what was on her mind. Was she feeling bad for him? Like he'd missed out on being a part of something?

Hell, he had—as a kid. But Kyle had given up

wanting to belong to the Bingham family years ago. He didn't need them or their acceptance.

He again glanced at Milla, wondering why she looked so thoughtful.

Kyle had said bloodlines didn't make a family, and Milla supposed he was right. Just because he'd fathered her baby didn't mean he'd be a part of the child's life. Did it?

But she still had to tell him and give him the opportunity to choose to be involved with the baby or not. But recently, whenever they'd been together, the timing had been wrong.

She couldn't very well blurt out the news in the hospital cafeteria, where they'd both been exhausted, or in front of Dylan. But where and when should she tell him?

Not over a candlelit dinner. News of a baby wasn't something Kyle would want to celebrate.

"I'd still like to have that talk with you," she said. "When the time is right."

"Sure," Kyle said. "Maybe after lunch."

She glanced in the back seat and saw the eager grin on Dylan's face. No, not after lunch.

"It doesn't have to be today," she said. But she had a feeling once she got it off her chest she'd feel much better about things.

She needed to tell him soon.

Very soon.

* * *

After they'd eaten lunch and had their fill of ice-cold lemonade, Milla made a pit stop in the ladies' rest room—something she'd been doing more often lately, thanks to an expanding uterus that pushed against her bladder.

As she walked out the exit and into the bright afternoon sunshine, she spotted Mari Bingham talking to a handsome man who looked a bit familiar, although Milla didn't know why.

They stood off to the side, away from the crowd. For a moment, Milla wondered if Mari might have a special friend or lover—until she caught the serious expressions on their faces.

She wouldn't have thought anything of it, had Mari not seemed so tense and so obviously bothered by the man. Should Milla interrupt? Interfere? Or just let Mari handle things on her own?

About the time Milla had decided to continue on her way, the dark-haired man strode across the grass and headed toward the parking lot, leaving Mari alone—and looking miserable.

"Is everything all right?" Milla asked as she approached the director she'd grown to respect.

Mari blew out a sigh. "Yeah." It was the kind of statement that could be taken either way.

"That man looked familiar," Milla said. "I think I've seen him before."

"You probably have."

Milla tried to put her finger on where and when.

Maybe she'd seen his face on television. "Hey, isn't he that used car salesman with the sleazy TV commercial?"

"No. That was Detective Bryce Collins. He had some questions for me, but it was more like an interrogation."

"Why is that?"

"He believes I'm involved in that black market Orcadol ring."

"He must not know you very well," Milla said.

Mari turned, caught her eye. "Actually, he does know me. Or at least he did. That's what has me so frustrated."

"I don't understand."

Mari paused for a moment, as though trying to voice an explanation. But she merely said, "Bryce and I go back many years."

"So, if that's the case, why would the detective think you're involved in something illegal?"

"Because of my involvement with Dr. Ricardo Phillipe."

"The man you've been working with on the research facility?"

Mari nodded. "Ricardo is a brilliant man who was involved in the early research of Orcadol. He also came close to losing his license a few years back because of drug and alcohol abuse."

Milla had to agree with the detective. Dr. Phillipe didn't seem like the kind of man Mari should have gotten involved with. Milla usually tried to keep her reactions from showing on her face, but a frown and a furrowed brow must have given her surprise away.

Mari, apparently, thought an explanation was needed. "Ricardo was critically injured in a car accident that claimed the life of his wife and three-year-old daughter. He was not only devastated by his grief, but in severe pain for months on end."

"Is that when his drug problem started?"

Mari crossed her arms. "I won't make excuses for his trouble in the past, but he's straightened out his life and been clean and sober for five years."

"I'm glad to hear that," Milla said, although she couldn't help wondering whether Dr. Phillipe was involved with the black market drug ring, in spite of what her mentor believed.

"I consider Ricardo Phillipe a good friend, as well as a colleague. And I trust him completely."

Obviously, Detective Collins wasn't as understanding or as forgiving.

Milla hoped Mari's trust wasn't misplaced. "So it was your contact with Dr. Phillipe that caused the detective to sit up and take note?"

"Yes. But Bryce also knows the clinic and research facility hit financial straits when several donors pulled back on funds." A light breeze kicked up, and Mari brushed a strand of hair from her cheek. "In the detective's mind I'm a suspect. And he seems to think if he harasses me enough, I'll give myself away."

"If he knew you before, I'd think he'd give you the benefit of the doubt."

Mari slowly shook her head. "Time has a way of changing things—and people."

"Hey, Mom!" Dylan cried out. "You're gonna miss the three-legged race, and me and Kyle are gonna win!"

"I'll be right there, honey!" Milla called back. Then she returned her attention to Mari. "Things will work out."

"I know they will, eventually. Thanks for your optimism." Mari managed a smile. "By the way, Joe Canfield called. They've dropped the lawsuit."

"Thank goodness. That's a huge relief."

"I thought you'd be happy."

"You have no idea," Milla said, blowing out a sigh. "But listen, Mari, if you ever need to talk to anyone—"

"I appreciate your support." Mari gave her a pat on the shoulder, then said, "I'll let you get back to your family."

Back to her family?

Milla, Dylan and Kyle weren't a family. But she supposed it didn't matter and refrained from correcting her friend.

To be honest, it felt kind of nice to think of Kyle and Dylan as a part of her family. And if she were one to believe in fairy tales and happily-ever-after, she'd cross her fingers, toes and everything bendable if it would help to make Kyle fall in love with her.

But it would be a wasted effort.

Someday her prince might come, but he wouldn't

be wearing a stethoscope and driving a shiny, black BMW.

And his last name wouldn't be Bingham.

As the sun moved across the summer sky, Kyle and Dylan competed in every single game and contest, sometimes making a showing, other times failing miserably. But they always came away with a smile that warmed Milla's heart.

They lost the egg-tossing contest when Kyle missed a ten-foot toss and collected a splatter of yolk and shell on what appeared to be a brand-new Tommy Bahama shirt.

"No big deal," Kyle had said, when Milla mentioned it.

As he and Dylan prepared to enter the three-legged race, Milla couldn't help but offer a suggestion. "There's a trick to this particular competition. Maybe you two should practice."

"Good idea." Kyle took Dylan aside and tutored him in the fine art of gunnysacks and three-legged races, until the whistle blew, signaling the start of the event.

While the contestants lined up on the grassy field, listening to rules and being handed their burlap bags, Milla stood on the sidelines, ready to cheer her team to victory.

"Hello, there."

Milla turned to see one of the lab techs at her side, an older woman she'd seen but never met.

"I'm Sarah Dunlap," the older woman said. "I work in the lab."

Milla introduced herself and extended a hand. "I'm a midwife working out of the clinic."

"I'm sorry for horning in," Sarah said, "but years ago, I used to live next door to Sally and Kyle—I mean Dr. Bingham." The woman chuckled. "I never will get used to calling that boy 'Doctor.' He was sweet as the dickens, and quite a little hell-raiser."

"I'd like to have known him as a boy," Milla said, thinking Kyle must have been a lot like Dylan.

"He was a loving child, but he sure did have a penchant for mischief. Caused his mother a few gray hairs. But look at him now."

Yes, look at him.

Milla studied Kyle, who was teaching her son how to be a man by setting a fine example.

The afternoon breeze rustled his golden hair, making him look like a Viking poised on the helm of his ship, and as he braced himself to run with Dylan, corded muscles tightened in his tanned legs.

"Kyle has certainly grown up to be a good man," Sarah said.

That he had.

But had he begun to mellow? To want more than a no-strings-attached relationship? Had he become his own person? Or was he merely a younger version of his playboy father?

Kyle had offered to help with Dylan, in a big-brotherly way. And he was doing an incredible job of it. He'd also come to her defense with the Canfields, convincing them to drop that lawsuit.

Maybe there was hope.

Hope for what? she asked herself, demanding honesty.

All right. She hoped there was a chance that something lasting could actually develop between her and Kyle.

Did she dare hope they could renew their...their what? Affair? Relationship?

As the crowd began to cheer, Milla realized the race had started while she was daydreaming.

"Go, Dylan and Kyle!" she yelled through cupped hands. "You can do it!"

And as the brothers hobbled over the finish line to claim their first-place ribbon, warmth flooded Milla's heart and soul.

Her team...her family had won.

Okay, so they weren't a family. But they were all she had to call her own. And for the time being, she'd lay claim to both of them.

She just wished this day could last forever.

But all good things came to an end. And so did the picnic. Karla's committee began to clean up, and the chuck wagon people packed up their wares and headed out of the parklike grounds.

As Milla climbed back into Kyle's car, tired yet happy, she thanked the man who'd made the hospital picnic extra special. "It was a wonderful day, and we had a great time."

Kyle slid her a crooked smile. "Me, too. I haven't had this kind of fun in years."

"I haven't had this much fun in my whole *life*," Dylan exclaimed. "And look at all our prizes."

They'd taken one blue ribbon and three whites, not to mention a bag of candy from the Paul Bunyan and Babe the Blue Ox piñatas the hospital board had provided for the children.

"There's a college baseball game in Lexington late Tuesday afternoon," Kyle said. "And I've got tickets. Would you and Dylan like to go?"

"Oh, wow!" Dylan said. "Please say yes, Mom!"

How could she say no? She'd have to get someone to cover for her, though. And she'd been shuffling her schedule a lot lately. Maybe it would be better to let the brothers go alone this time.

"I'm not sure if I can take the time off," she told Kyle. "But if you and Dylan want to make it a boys' night out, that's fine with me."

"Yay!" Dylan shrieked from the back seat, convincing her she'd made the right decision. "And it's only gonna be us guys."

The developing relationship had done Dylan a world of good. Kyle, too, she suspected.

Would Kyle be as willing to bond with their baby as he'd been with Dylan?

Or would he, like her father and his, leave mother and child to fend for themselves?

Milla didn't want to believe that. Kyle had changed

from the rebellious kid of his youth. Hadn't his old neighbor said as much?

"It's going to be way cool going to the baseball game with you, Kyle."

"I'm looking forward to it, too, buddy."

Milla relaxed in her seat. See? Kyle wanted to spend time with Dylan alone. And he was looking forward to the game. Kyle wouldn't desert Dylan.

And Milla was crazy for even worrying about it.

Chapter Fourteen

Kyle sat on the living room sofa, drinking an ice-cold beer and watching baseball on TV.

It had been a great day, and he still couldn't get over the fact that he'd actually enjoyed himself, playing what once had seemed like a bunch of stupid games.

Who would have guessed?

Apparently, Milla and Dylan brought out a playful side in him—something he hadn't known he had.

He took a swig from the longneck bottle and savored the malt taste as he watched a game between the Braves and the Reds. The score was tied, and it looked like they'd go into extra innings.

As the catcher called a time-out and went to speak to the pitcher on the mound, the phone rang.

He picked it up. "Hello."

"Kyle?" the man asked.

"Yeah. Who's this?"

"Ron Bingham."

Kyle nearly dropped the bottle he held in his hand. Ron was Mari's dad, his father's brother. And the Bingham patriarch. Kyle's mom had pointed Ron out once or twice, so Kyle knew who he was, what he looked like. But he hadn't ever talked to his uncle before, and the call came as a complete surprise.

Never at a loss for words, Kyle struggled for a response, for some reason. He finally asked, "What can I do for you?"

"We're having a small get-together at my mother's house, and I thought it would be nice if you came by."

His ability to make a snappy comment returned. "I've never been on a Bingham party guest list. Why now?"

"I thought it was time we got a chance to meet, maybe get to know each other."

Quite frankly, it seemed like a few years too late. But Kyle found it hard to say no and even harder to make the kind of smart-ass comeback that had become his trademark—and his first line of defense.

He tempered his response. "Is there something in particular you want to discuss?"

"Yes and no. My daughter speaks highly of you. She says you're a great doctor and will be a fine addition to the staff, if you decide to build a practice in Merlyn County.''

"I appreciate that," Kyle said. Mari had indicated her respect on several occasions. Her acceptance, at least on a professional basis, was a start. But it wasn't enough to keep him in town any longer than for his residency. Of course, there was no reason to mention that to his uncle.

Kyle would be lying if he said Ron's call didn't mean anything to him. He just wished it didn't mean so much.

"I know your dad wasn't always there for you," Ron said, "and I guess the family hasn't been, either. But I thought it was time we tried to make amends."

Kyle wasn't sure there was a way to make things right, although he appreciated the man's efforts. "Sure, Ron. Dinner sounds fine."

"By the way, Tuesday would have been your father's forty-fourth birthday. It's usually a difficult day for my mother, so we try to gather and keep her company." Ron cleared his throat. "The significance of the day may not come up, but if it does, I didn't want you to be surprised. Or uneasy."

"I understand," Kyle said. "What time should I stop by?"

"Six o'clock. Do you need directions?"

Hell, no. Everyone knew where the Bingham estate was located. "I'll be there."

When the call ended, Kyle took a long swig of beer, still somewhat amazed at what had happened.

A crack sounded over the TV, and he looked up to
see a rookie slam a line drive to the first-base man,
as Luke Holbrook slid into home.

All right, Braves!

He loved baseball.

Baseball.

Oh, crap. He had tickets to the college game in
Lexington. And he'd already invited Dylan.

He hated to back out on the kid, but it was the first
time he'd been invited to a Bingham family function.
And those old childhood hurts begged to be healed.

As far as he could see, there was only one option.
He had to call and cancel with Dylan. The boy would
be disappointed, but Kyle would make it up to him.

Somehow.

The birthday dinner at the Bingham estate was a
big deal.

And far more important than Kyle wanted it to be.

Dylan had yawned several times during dinner,
and, just after seven o'clock, Milla had finally insisted
he take a bath. She figured he was winding down
from an exciting day in the fresh air and sunshine.
And quite frankly, she was exhausted, too. She'd
showered an hour ago and already put on her night-
gown, an unbelievably comfy piece of white cotton
and torn lace that had seen better days.

"That country-and-western music special is on
TV," her mom said. "Want to watch it with me?"

"No, I'm going to turn in early." Not only was

Milla tired, but she wanted to get her thoughts together, because she intended to tell Kyle about the baby tomorrow.

He'd agreed to talk to her, although they hadn't set a day and time. Maybe he would meet her someplace quiet where they could speak in private. Or better yet, she could drive over to his house, where they would be alone. Then she could leave and let him think about things.

It didn't seem like a bad plan, especially since she wouldn't have to speculate about his reaction any longer. She'd know, firsthand.

Again, the infamous Billy Bingham reared his ghostly head. Milla realized Kyle wasn't like his father, but she couldn't seem to ditch the multitude of warnings her mother had given her.

Would Kyle abandon her and the baby she carried—a little boy or girl they created one star-spinning summer night?

The phone rang, and she answered on the second ring. It was Kyle. She couldn't help but smile at the sound of his voice.

They chatted for a moment, and then he said, "I need to talk to Dylan. Something important has come up, and I can't make that ball game. Can I speak to him?"

"Sure." She knew Dylan would feel bad about missing the game, but she was glad Kyle wanted to explain it himself.

Milla called her son, who hurried to snatch the phone from her hands.

"Hello?" The glimmer in his eyes slowly faded, as he listened to what Kyle said.

Milla longed to listen in, to be a part of the conversation, but she only had Dylan's words and expressions to go by.

His brow furrowed, and his lip quivered. "I understand. Uh-huh. No. Okay. Bye."

As the boy hung up the phone, tears rolled down his face, and he brushed them away with the blue flannel sleeve of his pajamas. "We aren't going to the ball game Tuesday."

"Why not?" Milla knew there had to be a good reason.

"Kyle has to go to a party with some friends."

That wasn't the excuse Milla had expected, and quite frankly, it didn't fly with her.

A party? He canceled with Dylan because of a party with his friends?

Always the footloose bachelor, wasn't he?

"What was that all about?" her mother asked, from her front row seat at the Grand Ol' Opry.

Only the first of many disappointments, Milla wanted to say. But she bit her lip and held back the truth, unwilling to give her mom any more ammo to use against the Bingham clan. Although, if truth be told, she couldn't figure out why she was protecting Kyle. She would give him a piece of her mind, if he were standing in front of her.

"Something important came up," Milla lied. "And Kyle isn't going to be able to take Dylan to the ball game in Lexington."

"That's too bad," Sharon said, turning her attention to the young fiddle player who had her sitting on the edge of the green vinyl recliner.

"I'm sure he'll make it up to him," Milla said, her lips tightening with the excuse that didn't satisfy her any more than it had Dylan.

Maybe it was time to curtail the relationship between Kyle and Dylan. Her son didn't need the emotional roller coaster ride, not if Kyle would change their plans whenever he got a better offer.

She followed Dylan into his room. "Are you okay?"

"Yeah." His red-rimmed eyes suggested otherwise. "Kyle said there would be other games."

And other disappointments, Milla feared. But she didn't need to mention that to the boy, not when his little heart was on the chopping block.

She wanted to defend Kyle, but how could she? He'd brushed Dylan aside because of some stupid party with his friends.

As her son cried into his pillow, she stroked his flannel-clad back and sat with him for a while.

Before long, he sucked up his tears like a man. "I'm okay now."

"Good. I'm glad."

"It's just that I was looking forward to going. But he said we could do something else together. Soon."

"I know," she said, although she wasn't sure she could trust that Kyle would make good on his promise. She brushed a kiss across the boy's forehead. "Good night, honey. I love you."

"I love you, too."

Then she excused herself and went to her room. Alone. And even though her mom was still in the living room, watching TV, the maternal warnings filled the small bedroom.

Be careful, honey. The Binghams will turn on you.

Well, she didn't know about all the Binghams. But it seemed as though Billy and Kyle had been cut from the same bolt of silk.

Milla admonished herself for not listening to her mother, for not being better prepared for that last phone call. Kyle might make it up to Dylan, but Milla wouldn't be as easy to convince. He'd dumped her son because of a party.

As she slid between the cool, cotton sheets, she didn't expect to sleep well. Her rest would be interrupted by dreams of apples that didn't fall far from the tree and leopards that didn't change their spots.

Kyle felt badly about canceling the trip to Lexington with Dylan, especially since the kid had sounded disappointed on the phone.

He wasn't sure what kind of schedule Milla had on Sunday morning, but he thought it might be a good idea to stop by her house and make sure they both

understood that he'd do his best to make it up
to the boy.

Of course, he wasn't about to go into all that childhood baggage he carried, but he would try and explain
why he couldn't go to the ball game.

Somehow.

Maybe he'd tell her he didn't want to disappoint
his grandmother, a woman he'd never actually met.

No, maybe it was best to keep the Binghams out
of the discussion.

He'd kept his disappointment and pain a secret for
years. Hell, his mother didn't even know how bad he
felt about being an outcast. But he'd had his reasons
for not leveling with her.

He'd always known she'd loved his father. And on
several occasions he'd suspected she might have accepted Billy's playboy ways and maintained a discreet relationship with the man, whenever he found
time for her.

No, the pain Kyle had carried because of the
Binghams' lack of interest was a burden he'd carried
alone. A burden he intended to keep to himself. It
was better to stick with the birthday-party-for-a-friend
excuse.

Oh, hell. He didn't know exactly what he'd say,
but he'd figure out something. He'd always been able
to think on his feet.

When he knocked on Milla's door, her mother answered. At five-four and with brunette hair and big
brown eyes, she resembled her daughter. But she

lacked Milla's effervescence and charm. And her dimpled smile.

"Is Milla here?"

"She'll be right back. She walked Dylan down the street. He's going to Sunday school with the neighbors who live around the corner. Would you like to come in?"

"Thank you." Kyle entered the dark, wood-paneled room and waited for his eyes to adjust. Why didn't the woman pull open the curtains? The room was depressing, as far as he was concerned.

"Have a seat," she said, indicating a tired sofa that had been covered with a floral slipcover. "I'm Sharon Johnson, Milla's mother."

"Kyle Bingham," he told her.

"I know. You look just like your daddy."

Did that comment require a thank-you? For some reason, he suspected she hadn't meant it as a compliment.

The woman studied him for a while, assessing him it seemed.

Well, maybe he ought to try and put some of her concerns aside. "I can't make up for Dylan not having a dad. Nor can I make up for the past. But I intend to be a part of my little brother's life."

"That's good," she said. "Lord knows he needs a man to take an interest in him. I just hope you won't tire of him."

Sharon didn't have to continue. Kyle knew what

she meant. The woman feared he'd bail out on Dylan,
like their father had bailed on the kids he'd fathered.

"You're going to have to judge me on my own
merits, not my father's."

"Fair enough, I guess." Milla's mother winced,
then rubbed the back of her neck.

"What's the matter?"

"Just that fool pain again." She sighed. "I had a
car accident a few years back and suffered a whiplash
that left me with some nerve damage. I'm in a lot of
pain most of the time."

"Have you seen a neurologist?" Kyle asked.

"I saw one once, but the insurance company refused to cover the referral." She shrugged. "Not
much I can do, except live with it."

"I'd like you to talk to Dr. Gardner. He's one of
the best neurosurgeons in the state. I'll give him a
heads-up and let him know I asked you to call."

She shook her head. "I'm sorry, Dr. Bingham. But
I just can't afford to pay for another office visit or
more tests. Since my insurance is so fussy, it would
be an out-of-pocket expense."

"It won't cost you a thing," Kyle said.

"Thanks for the offer, but I don't feel right about
taking charity."

"It's not charity. I'm sure Dr. Gardner will see you
free of charge, as a professional courtesy to me."

Sharon seemed to struggle with his generosity. Or
maybe with her pain.

"Do you like hurting?" he asked.

"Heavens, no. What kind of fool question is that?"

"Well, if there's a possibility that Dr. Gardner can provide a treatment or different medication that might help you, it makes me wonder why you'd refuse to see him."

"Why would he want to examine me? For free, I mean."

"Because he's a friend and a colleague."

"Well," she said, obviously struggling with the decision. "I appreciate you talking to him, and if he's agreeable, I'll see him. Thank you."

"I'll have his office give you a call on Monday morning to schedule an appointment."

Footsteps sounded on the walk, the screen door swung open and Milla entered the house. Kyle hoped she would see that he and her mother had reached an understanding of sorts. But when he looked in her eyes, he saw a flash of anger.

And absolutely no sign of a smile.

"What are you doing here?" Milla asked.

He hadn't been prepared for the sharp tone of her voice or the fire in her eyes. What was the problem? Did she dislike him dropping by without an invitation?

"I came by to talk to you," he said.

"About what?"

Tension crackled through the house like a wildfire, and he wasn't exactly sure why.

"What crawled into your breakfast cereal box?" he asked, unable to help the snippy retort.

She bristled. "Excuse me?"

Maybe it was her time of the month. Some women could benefit from one of the new treatments for PMS. Maybe Milla was one of them. "Let's start over. If you're mad about me stopping by without calling first—"

"I'm not." She crossed her arms and shifted her weight to one foot. "But I hope you have fun at your party on Tuesday evening."

He'd told her something important had come up. And he'd told Dylan it was a birthday party. What was Milla's problem?

His first impulse was to take the offense, like he'd always done in the past. But this was different. Milla was different. And he wanted to back up and start over. To get on her good side. "I'm sorry that the baseball game in Lexington won't work out, but I'll try to make it up to Dylan."

"That won't be necessary. He needs to learn to handle disappointment. And I'm sure a party with your friends is more important to you than a baseball game with a little boy."

Kyle glanced at Milla's mother, unable to read her tight-lipped expression. He wasn't prepared to defend himself, especially in front of an audience. "Come on, Milla. I'll make it up to him. You're going to have to trust me."

"Trust you?" Milla asked, her cheeks heating to keep pace with her temper. "To be a man of your word?"

"That's not fair."

Maybe it wasn't, but Milla didn't feel in charge of her emotions right now. She wanted to cry in frustration. She'd told herself that Kyle was different. And she'd even convinced herself that he might grow to love her.

But she'd been wrong.

And it was better to face the truth.

"Dylan adores you," she said, "but he doesn't need to have the rug jerked out from under him."

"Why don't you let me work this out with Dylan? You're getting all worked up over nothing."

All worked up? Over nothing?

How dare he patronize her! It wasn't just Dylan she hurt for. It was her own child. And herself.

She'd fallen in love with the man who'd fathered her baby. A man who would choose his friends and a party over a child who loved him.

"I'm not wound up. I'm just trying to protect Dylan." Actually, she was trying to protect them all.

"What's really bothering you, Milla?"

Nothing, she wanted to say. Everything. The hormones were doing a real number on her, jolting her maternal instincts into play. Making her heart go crazy and demanding she build a family and make things right.

"Level with me," he said. "What's the real issue here?"

"I'm pregnant, Kyle." The words left her mouth before she could even consider the ramifications. Before she could plan the proper way to tell him. Before she could consider everyone in the room.

Her mother jumped to her feet and shrieked, "You're what?"

Oh, Lord. Had she admitted that? Here?

Now she'd really done it. But it was too late to backpedal. "I'm pregnant. All right? An unwed mother. And it doesn't appear that I can offer my child any more than that."

Then she turned on her heel and walked out the door, picking up the pace and hoping the summer sun would lighten the load she carried. But the tears welled up in her eyes, and a sob caught her throat.

Talk about planning the perfect time to tell him. Milla had sure screwed up this time.

But so what? Kyle had shown his true colors.

And, unfortunately, so had she.

Kyle stood like a rusted tin soldier, unable to move or blink.

Milla was pregnant?

He looked at the stunned expression on her mother's face, wishing he were anywhere but here.

"Who's the father?" Sharon asked, snaring him with a hardened gaze.

How the hell did he know? Milla's words had blindsided him, shaking him to the bone.

They'd used condoms. But had they gotten careless? It was possible. He'd only had one thing on his mind that night, and frankly, the condoms had been a secondary thought. Had he and Milla become one of the failure statistics?

Kyle supposed he was the father, unless Milla had been pregnant when they met. Where the hell had she run off to? He had a few questions to ask her.

And a lot to consider.

Pregnant. A baby?

No wonder she was edgy.

"I asked who the father was," Sharon repeated, claws and fangs bared, ready to pounce on the man who'd taken advantage of her daughter.

"I don't know," he said. "I suppose it could be me."

"So what are you going to do about it?" Sharon asked.

How the heck did he know? The news had come at him like a shot in the dark. He had no idea how he felt or what to say.

Instead of responding, Kyle turned and walked out the door.

His only thought was to escape.

And to run like hell.

Chapter Fifteen

Milla marched through the sleepy neighborhood until her mind cleared and reality settled in.

Her secret was out.

And she'd blown the delivery.

She'd wanted so badly to have a heart-to-heart with Kyle, revealing her pregnancy in just the right way. Instead, she'd flipped out like a crazy woman.

And her mom had heard her blurt out the truth. Could she have botched up a conversation any worse?

Well, she couldn't very well wander the streets for the rest of her life. It was time to go home and face the music. To listen to a rapid-fire rendition of I-told-you-so.

As she turned the corner and made her way down

the cul-de-sac on which she lived, she noticed only one car in the driveway, her tired old Caprice Classic.

Kyle had left.

Well, what did she expect? Hearts and flowers? Tears of joy? She'd suspected that he might walk out the minute he learned the truth. And she'd been right.

Of course, the fact that her mother may have sped up the process couldn't be overlooked. But unloading on him, like Milla had done, had been a sneak attack. And she really couldn't blame him for wanting to duck and run, instead of withdrawing slowly as she'd expected.

Kyle Bingham had no intention of settling down or of being a husband or father. Hadn't he said as much on several occasions?

She trudged up the walk and into the house, like a remorseful little puppy who'd piddled on the carpet, and found her mother pacing the floor in her pink chenille housecoat and scruffy blue slippers.

"So, you couldn't listen to me or learn from your aunt's mistakes."

Milla wasn't going to assume the role of victim. And the sooner her mother got a few things straight, the better off they'd all be. She crossed her arms, taking a firm stand. "Listen, Mom. I lost my head a few minutes ago and blurted out something that was best said in private."

"You can say that again. Your crazed announcement took me by surprise. And ol' Billy Junior looked as though he'd been walloped over the head with a cast-iron skillet.''

Milla's resolve faltered, but only because of her mother's take on Kyle's reaction. She still had every intention of laying some ground rules and boundaries. ''That's enough, Mom. I'm pregnant, and I take full responsibility.''

''That man—''

''That man's name is Kyle, and he's the father of my baby.'' Milla stepped closer, taking complete charge of her life. ''Let's get something straight. I won't listen to you bad-mouth Kyle like you did his father. I chose to become involved with him, and I won't make excuses for it. I'm going to be an unwed mother. And you're going to be a grandmother. End of story.''

''You make it sound so easy—''

''I'm sure it will be far from easy. And there's no reason for me to believe that Kyle will be involved in my baby's life. But that's his choice. And it's also his loss.''

''How will you support yourself? We're struggling to get by as it is.''

''You don't have to worry about it, Mom. Supporting the baby, with or without Kyle's help, is my problem. And I won't discuss this with you again.''

''What do you mean by that?''

Bottled emotions clogged her throat. She loved her mother and didn't want to cause her any additional pain. But she also had to think of her unborn child.

"It means that I'm an adult now, Mom. And like it or not, you'll honor my decision to be the best mother a baby could ever want. And you'll keep your feelings about Kyle and his father to yourself."

"What if I can't do that?" she asked.

"Then you won't be a part of my baby's life. It's as simple as that. I won't raise this child under the same cloud of depression and bitterness that Dylan has always lived under."

Her mother fiddled with the worn lapel of her robe and furrowed her brow.

"Your anger and grief have been a burden for all of us," Milla said. "And I want this baby to know love and happiness."

Sharon's eyes bore the grief she'd yet to shed. "I loved my sister, more than you'll ever know."

"And she's gone." Milla turned and strode to the window. She opened the drapes, letting the morning sunlight flood the room. "This house is dark and dreary and better suited for a morgue than a home for growing children. And starting today, things are going to change."

"I didn't know you felt that way…I just…"

Milla strode across the room and wrapped her arms around her mother, pulling her close. "I love you, Mom. But the mourning period is over. It's time for all of us to start living."

Sharon leaned into the embrace, resting her head against Milla's, and started to cry. "I've become a bitter old woman, haven't I?"

A tear slipped down Milla's face, and she swiped it away. "You're not old. But it's time to let go of the resentment."

It might be easier said than done, but Milla was determined to create a warm and loving home for her baby.

Especially since she'd be the only person her baby could depend on to look out for its best interests.

When Kyle climbed into his car and drove away from Milla's house, there was just one thing on his mind—escape.

He had to get away from her mother's evil eye.

Away from Milla's startling revelation.

Away from whatever decision he'd be forced to make.

His once perfect life was spinning out of control, and he struggled to make sense of Milla's pregnancy announcement and what now seemed like a very uncertain future. Assuming Milla's baby was his—and he had no reason to believe otherwise—there'd be some big changes coming down the pike.

When he reached the edge of town, he proceeded to Bluebonnet Lane, where he could hide behind the fortress of his own four walls—walls he'd be climbing if he went home now.

No. Not home. Instead of turning right, he made a left and drove to the cemetery, although he had no idea why. Not really.

He hadn't been there since the day they buried

Jimmy Hoben. The day he'd promised his best friend that he'd find a way to cure kids like him from diseases that ravaged young bodies before their time.

Kyle parked the car and strolled the solemn setting, past pinwheels that decorated a child's grave, past faded plastic flowers left to honor a loved one. Past flags that adorned the graves of dead soldiers.

He found Jimmy's marker, a small inlaid piece of concrete that bore only his name. When Kyle went home, he'd make some calls, do what he could to give the boy who'd been his best friend, his only true friend, a more fitting memorial. Maybe something with fishing poles carved on the side. He'd think of something special. And far more appropriate.

Kyle said a graveside prayer, wishing Jimmy well. Telling him he missed not having someone to confide in. Then he turned and walked away. Rather than feeling better, he felt as though something had been missing, as though something was left unsaid.

As he neared a weeping willow that grew in the center of the grounds, he spotted the marble headstone that rose higher than the others, marking Gerard Bingham's place of rest. After Jimmy's funeral his mom had pointed out his grandfather's grave to him, but he hadn't cared. His only thought that day had been to go home, lock himself in his bedroom and turn up the volume on his stereo so that no one could hear him cry.

But he wasn't grieving today. At least, he didn't

think so; he couldn't be sure of the emotions that snowballed him from all sides.

He made the trek over green lawns that blanketed the graves of deceased Merlyn County residents. Gone but not forgotten, as one stone marker said.

He reached the polished marble pillar that bore the Bingham name, spotting the black, double-sided stone that was complete on only one side. "Gerard Joseph Bingham, 1910–1972."

To the left of the hand-carved words, room was left for his wife. "Myrtle Northrup Bingham, 1926—"

The date of death was blank.

He stood respectfully for a while, until the silver-gray stone to the left caught his eye—the one that bore his father's name.

William Richard Bingham, 1957–1994.

It was a single headstone. No space for a wife, since his father hadn't made room in his life for a special woman. The footloose bachelor hadn't made room for kids, either.

"I'd always felt as though you'd bailed out on me," Kyle spoke over the grave. "But your dying made it even worse."

His eyes grew misty, but he didn't cry. He held back the tears, but he couldn't hold back the words from that place where he'd kept them stored for years. "You were a selfish bastard—not with money. But you never opened your heart to anyone. Not a boy who needed you. And not even the woman who loved you until your dying day."

A flock of birds flew overhead, and the warm summer breeze seemed to whisper a reminder that only memories lived here. Happy ones for some people. But sad ones for him.

As much as Kyle had never wanted to follow in his father's footsteps, it seemed he had. And now he was forced to make a decision. Did he want to repeat history?

What a day this had turned out to be. For a guy who'd zipped in and out of life's fast lane like a stock car in the Daytona 500, Kyle had slammed into a concrete wall.

A baby.

He blew out a loud breath, then shook his head. Now what? He'd always done his best to avoid even the thought of fatherhood, but he would step up to the plate—financially.

Emotionally, too, he supposed, although that might be tough to do. He'd never been a touchy-feely type of guy. And kids needed that sort of thing.

He glanced at his father's headstone. "You never set any kind of example for me."

Was his father sorry? If so, Kyle would forgive the man, but his father couldn't speak, and Kyle would never know for sure. But one thing seemed clear. If he held on to the anger, he'd never be free.

Kyle closed his eyes, releasing the resentment and forgiving his father. For the first time in his life, he realized something important. And monumental.

The one granting forgiveness was the one who came out on top.

"Goodbye, Dad."

Then Kyle turned and walked away. Back to his car. Back to an aimless drive for peace of mind.

He wasn't sure what kind of father he'd make, but there was no way in hell he'd let his kid grow up without a dad to turn to, not after learning firsthand how difficult that made things for a child.

His child. He blew out another heavy sigh. The thought of parenthood made him skittish, but he'd better get used to the idea. He and Milla had created a baby, a unique, living, breathing genetic combination of the two of them that would soon enter the world and draw breath.

Would the baby be a boy or girl? Would it look like Milla, with her chocolate-colored hair and expressive brown eyes?

Would she nurse their newborn, holding it close and whispering words of love? He hoped so. That's what he would want for a child of his.

Of course, he had no doubt Milla would make a great mother. He'd seen the way she'd lovingly tended the little boy who would go home with the Canfields. Seen the way she'd stuck by Kyle's side, even though she looked tired enough to drop in her tracks. And he'd seen her with Dylan, the motherless boy she intended to adopt.

Yes, Milla was the kind of woman who'd make a great mother. And a wonderful wife.

A wife?

Yeah, he could see Milla as a wife—his wife.

But could he see himself as a husband? The kind of guy who looked forward to going home each night?

His father had never been able to make that commitment, and for a while, Kyle had felt the same way. He'd followed his father's example without realizing it.

But would Kyle be content, day after day, to see the same smiling face across the table? To make love to the same warm and willing woman each night, to wake in her arms every morning?

He would—if that woman was Milla.

No one else had ever touched his heart the way she had. No other woman had infiltrated his dreams, his thoughts.

Kyle wasn't sure what he felt for Milla, as powerful as it was. He'd always figured that lust had done a real number on him, making him blind to any other woman but her. But lust had nothing to do with the overwhelming urge to protect and shelter both her and their child.

Did he love her? He wasn't sure, since he'd never given romance and forever any consideration. But if what he felt for Milla wasn't love, it had to be something pretty darn close.

Kyle made a U-turn at the corner of Cassidy and Flint, then drove back to where all the confusion had hit the fan, where a myriad of emotions had been unleashed.

There was no escaping this time. Kyle needed to talk to Milla, to see her face-to-face. They had some decisions to make about their baby, their future—if she or her mom didn't throw him out on his ear first.

Ten minutes later he parked in front of Milla's house and climbed from the car. The place was quiet, except for the murmur of a church service on TV. He sure hoped the televangelist was preaching about love and forgiveness today. A hell-and-damnation-filled message might set Milla and her mother off and un- leash a hail of fire and brimstone—all of it aimed at him.

Determined to speak to Milla alone, Kyle walked up to the porch and rapped on the aluminum door. Through the screen, he could see her mother sitting on the sofa. The woman saw him, too, but didn't im- mediately speak. Of course, she didn't glare at him, either, the way she had nearly an hour before. Thank goodness for that. Score one for the TV preacher.

And one for the man upstairs.

Oh, boy. If Kyle married Milla, Sharon Johnson would be his mother-in-law. Yet even *that* didn't frighten him off, as it might have—before Milla had burrowed deep into his heart.

"You'd better answer the door, Milla," the older woman said. "It's for you."

The pretty midwife who made Kyle go all sappy inside entered the living room and spotted him through the screen. Her eyes widened and her steps slowed.

"Hi. I didn't expect to see you again." She ran a hand through the sable strands of her hair. "I mean, this soon. I'm sorry about the way I blew up…"

He opened the dark screen that separated them. "Will you come with me?"

She nodded. "I'll, uh, go get my purse."

As Milla left the room, leaving him standing just inside the door, her mother rose from her seat and approached him. "I apologize for my outburst. I, uh, was surprised to hear about the baby and reacted without thinking."

Kyle knew she'd carried those anti-Bingham, anti-Billy sentiments for years. And he figured her apology had been difficult to make.

"The news came as a surprise to me, too." He offered her a smile. "I meant what I said about me not being the same kind of man that my father was."

She nodded.

"And I meant what I said about Dr. Gardner," Kyle added. "I'm going to talk to him about you on Monday morning."

"Thank you," Sharon said. "I appreciate that."

When Milla returned with a small black bag that hung from a long strap on her shoulder, Sharon returned to her seat and the televised service she'd been watching.

"Come on," Kyle said, as he led Milla outside to the car and opened the passenger door.

She slid inside, then looked up at him with those big brown eyes that turned his heart every which way but loose. ''Where are we going?''

''I don't know. But it's time we had that little chat you've been talking about.''

Chapter Sixteen

Kyle held his front door open as Milla stepped inside the simple home that no longer felt adequate for his needs.

She cleared her throat. "I'm really sorry about blowing up at you like that. I'd wanted to pick the right time to tell you about the baby, but when you canceled that ball game—"

"Wait a minute," Kyle said, placing his hands gently upon Milla's shoulders. "First of all, Ron Bingham called me and invited me to a family get-together on Tuesday night. That might not sound important to you…" He paused, unsure of how much of his old baggage to bare. But when Milla caught his gaze, she peered into his heart, or at least it felt that way, and he no longer wanted any secrets between them.

"They don't include you very often, do they?" she asked.

"They've never included me in anything." His voice betrayed a boyish vulnerability, but he didn't try to shrug off the childhood disappointment or cover it up. He intended to lay his feelings on the line—all of them.

She cupped his jaw, offering compassion and understanding. He took ahold of her wrist, kissed the palm, then returned her hand to his cheek and held it in place.

"I'm sorry, Kyle. I assumed you'd been invited to some wild, adult party that was far more exciting than a ball game with a little boy. And I couldn't bear to have Dylan tossed aside like that, like…"

"Like you were tossed aside?" he asked, sensing someone had disappointed her.

She nodded. "My dad took off without a backward glance, and, if I let it, the rejection and abandonment still hurts."

"Ah, Milla." Kyle pulled her close, held her against him, trying to absorb her sadness and pain. "We've both had to deal with some of the same things. But that doesn't mean our kids will."

Our kids? Milla lifted her head from his chest. "What do you mean by *our kids?*"

"I mean Dylan and our baby." He brushed a kiss

across her brow. "And any other kids God blesses us with."

"You want us to be a family?" Her luminous brown eyes searched his gaze, finding a connection to his heart.

And at that very moment he knew without a doubt that he wanted to spend the rest of his life with this woman. "I love you, Milla."

Tears welled in her eyes, and her bottom lip quivered.

"I want to marry you."

"Because of the baby?" she asked.

"Because I love you. Because I want to sleep with you each night and wake with you in my arms every morning. I want to be your husband and the father of your children." He slid her a crooked grin. "But because of the *baby,* I think we ought to pass on planning a big wedding and speed things up."

"Are you sure?" she asked. "I don't want to tie you down."

Kyle laughed. "I'd love to be shackled to you for the rest of my life."

Milla wrapped her arms around his neck, eyes sparkling like two Hershey kisses. "I love you, too, Kyle."

His heart swelled, and he kissed her with all the love in his heart, all the hope in his soul.

He thrust his tongue deep in her mouth, opening the floodgates and unleashing the passion that flowed between them. Her kiss drove him wild, and her touch sent heat coursing through his blood, filling him with a demanding sense of urgency. He wanted her—now. And he wanted *only* her for the rest of his life.

Kyle slid a hand under the cotton of her T-shirt, felt her body react as his fingers skimmed her skin and found her breast. As he palmed the soft mound through her bra, her nipple hardened at his touch. She sucked in a breath, then worked feverishly to unbuckle his belt. She unhooked his waistband and unzipped his slacks, letting him know that she wanted him as desperately as he wanted her.

He thought about taking her here, in the living room—on the floor. And he might do that someday. But not now. Not when he meant to celebrate their love and their future.

"Come with me," he said, leading her into the bedroom.

When they neared his bed, she dropped his hand, just long enough to slip the soft cotton fabric of her shirt over her head and to unsnap her shorts and slide them past her hips.

When she stood before him in a lace bra and panties, his breath caught. "You're beautiful, Milla. What did I ever do to deserve you?"

"You allowed me to see the real man inside of you. And you opened your heart to me." She reached for the buttons of his shirt, undoing them, then slid the sleek blue fabric from his shoulders.

"I'm going to spend the rest of my life loving you," he said, brushing a kiss across her brow.

She removed her bra and let it drop to the floor, revealing the breasts he longed to taste and tease. And as she pressed herself to him, skin to skin, she rubbed against his erection, fanning his desire with her own. A low groan formed in his mouth.

He lifted her in his arms, then laid her on the bed and hovered over her, braced to offer everything he had, body and soul.

When she slid her fingers through his hair and drew his mouth to hers, he was lost in a swirl of heat and passion. He loved her with his hands, with his kiss, until his heart nearly burst from his chest and his arousal demanded release.

Milla savored each touch, each flick of Kyle's tongue, until she was wild with need. As his erection pressed against her, she opened for him. "I want you inside of me. Where you belong."

And where he wanted to be. He entered her, and she arched up to meet him, matching each of his thrusts with her own. Never had she felt so vulnerable yet so powerful.

The loving rhythm reached a mountainous peak, and a gripping climax burst forth like the shattering of stars into a million tiny sparkles. She cried out with the first wave of an orgasm that rocked her soul, and he shuddered in release.

They lay there for a while, sharing the ebb and flow, giving and taking, loving and being loved. And they basked in the afterglow of the star-bursting climax, celebrating a joining that promised forever.

"I love you, Milla. And I can't believe how easy that is to admit." Kyle ran a hand along the curve of her hip. "And do you know what? This is the first day of the rest of our lives."

Milla wasn't sure what the future held, but knowing that Kyle loved her, that they would face the world together, filled her with peace and contentment.

She smiled at the man she loved, the father of her baby. "So this is what 'And they lived happily ever after' means."

"You've got that right." Then Kyle took her in his arms and loved her all over again.

Kyle's black BMW maneuvered easily along the winding road that led to the Bingham estate.

A day before, he'd called Ron and asked if he could bring the woman who would soon be his wife and the boy who would be their son. It no longer mattered that Kyle was accepted; he wanted that acceptance for his entire family.

"Of course," Ron had said. "We'd like to meet them, too."

Kyle mentioned Dylan's relationship to the Binghams, although he wasn't sure why. Maybe because the boy looked so much like him and their father. And maybe because he hoped the Binghams would acknowledge another of Billy's illegitimate offspring.

As they neared the sprawling estate, Kyle glanced across the seat at Milla, and she smiled, offering her love and support.

How had he ever gotten along without her in his life?

"Wow," Dylan said from his seat in the back, gazing at the house where Myrtle Bingham lived alone. "I wonder if she ever gets lost in there. That place is really big."

It was. And Kyle couldn't curb his curiosity. In the past, he would have wanted to attend the dinner by himself, in case anyone snubbed him or made some kind of comment about his illegitimacy. But tonight, with Milla at his side, it no longer mattered.

It felt good to put away the old pains and hurts. And it felt good to be a team, a family.

"Are we the first ones here?" Milla asked. "I don't see any other cars."

"I guess." Kyle glanced at his watch. They'd arrived right on time. "Ron said to be here at six."

As they piled from the car, Dylan asked, "Can I ring the bell?"

Kyle laughed. "Sure. Go ahead."

Dylan sprinted up the tiled stairway that led to the front door, and Kyle reached for Milla's hand. He gave it a squeeze, happy to have her at his side—where she belonged.

She blessed him with another dimpled smile that banished all signs of the minor case of nervousness that had plagued him since his uncle's call.

By the time they climbed the steps and reached Dylan, Myrtle Bingham, the silver-haired matriarch of the Bingham clan, was waiting to greet them at the door. She welcomed them into her home.

The attractive woman who'd once been a New England debutante smiled warmly. "I thought it might be nice if we had a chance to meet first, so I called and asked Ron and the others to come a bit later. I hope you don't mind."

Kyle didn't. He wanted to have some time with his grandmother, a woman who'd been instrumental in starting the first midwifery service in Merlyn County and the Janice Foster Memorial Midwifery Clinic, which had been named after a friend of hers who'd died in childbirth.

Some folks in the community continued to criticize the late Gerard Bingham for his ruthlessness in business, but no one ever bad-mouthed his wife.

Myrtle led them through the marble-tiled foyer and into the living room, tastefully decorated in expensive shades of beige and cream. Kyle suspected the sculptures and paintings that adorned the room were originals. And no doubt pricey.

"Won't you please take a seat?" She indicated an ivory brocade sofa.

Two gift-wrapped packages sat on the glass coffee table, one bright green and the other sporting brightly colored rainbows and a big red bow.

"You have a lovely home," Milla said.

"Thank you." Myrtle sat in a beige wing chair. "I'd wanted to meet you years ago, Kyle. But I felt that it was your father's place to introduce you to me.

Then, after he passed away, you'd gone off to college.''

''I'm glad we finally got the chance to meet,'' Kyle said.

Myrtle turned her attention to Dylan, then looked at Kyle. ''Your son looks a lot like you, and you both favor your father.''

''Thanks,'' Kyle said, accepting her compliment.

Obviously, Ron had told his mother about her youngest grandson and about Kyle and Milla's adoption plans.

''Billy was always a happy, free spirit, much like his own father,'' Myrtle said, as though offering an explanation for her son's lifestyle.

Kyle nodded, not about to agree or argue.

''He would have been forty-four years old today.'' She bore a wistful look in her eye. ''The plane crash was a real tragedy, but in my heart, I knew Billy was destined to live fast and die young. Don't ask me how I knew that.''

Probably because he'd lived life so recklessly, Kyle figured, but he kept that thought to himself. Instead he said, ''I'm glad you invited us this evening.''

''I should have insisted that we make the effort sooner, and I apologize for not doing so.''

Kyle wished she had made the effort, too, although he wasn't sure whether he would have appreciated it as much as he did today. ''The timing is probably better, now that I have a family of my own.''

''Maybe so.'' The graceful woman reached for the

smaller of the two gift-wrapped boxes on the coffee table, then handed it to Kyle. "I have something I'd like to give you."

He accepted it, fingering it carefully. "Thank you."

"Open it," his grandmother said.

And he did. Inside, he found a black onyx ring.

"It was your father's," she said. "And your grandfather's before that. I'd like for you to have it."

The ring was a symbol of what she offered him—the acceptance he'd craved all of his life. Even when he'd scoffed at the legitimate side of the family, it had only been to mask his pain.

Kyle fingered the gold, handcrafted heirloom, then slipped it on his right hand, accepting his grandmother's generosity—and what his dad could no longer offer.

A sense of relief swept through his heart, freeing him from the old aches and disappointments. "Thank you."

"Your father would have wanted you to have it. He'd always said you would make something of yourself one day." The silver-haired woman smiled. "I doubt he could take much credit for your raising, though."

No, Kyle had to give his mother all the credit for that. She'd been the one who'd loved him, who'd sat up with him while he was sick. The one who'd gone to school and had meetings with the principal, the school psychologist and numerous frustrated teachers.

"I was lucky to have a wonderful mother," he said, unwilling to let his past resentments mar the future. He glanced at the ring that verified his acceptance into the family. "Your gift means a lot to me, Mrs. Bingham."

"I suppose it's a bit late to start using more familiar terms, like Grandma, although I'd certainly be comfortable with it. But I'd much rather you call me Myrtle than Mrs. Bingham."

He'd never experienced having a grandparent, and it seemed odd to have one now. But her words had touched him, more than he thought possible, triggering emotions he didn't realize he had. "I suppose, as our relationship grows, 'Grandma' might pop out every now and again."

Myrtle chuckled, then turned to Dylan. "I have something for you, too, dear."

The boy burst into a happy grin and looked at the other gift resting on the coffee table. And when his grandmother presented the package to him, he tore off the bright red bow and ripped open the colorful paper.

"Wow," he said, as he withdrew a baseball and a mitt that had been oiled and broken in. The fact that both ball and mitt had been used, didn't seem to faze Dylan. "Thank you, Grandma."

Myrtle beamed. "It was your father's. He played shortstop for Merlyn County High."

"He was a Lion?" Dylan asked. "Cool. I'm going to be a Lion someday, too."

The doorbell rang, announcing the arrival of the first of Kyle's extended family.

"That's probably Ron," Myrtle said. "He'll let himself in."

And he did. The CEO of Bingham Enterprises was a handsome man in his fifties, with salt-and-pepper hair, and a well-trimmed beard and mustache. He extended a hand to Kyle, welcoming him into the family as warmly as Myrtle had.

Mari arrived next, offering both Kyle and Milla a hug. "I'm glad you could join us."

While Ron offered everyone drinks, Mari's brother Geoff entered the living room with his wife, Cecilia.

Soon Kyle was drawn into the family, into the fold. And even more heartwarming was the way in which everyone spoke to Dylan, making the child feel as though he'd been born and raised in this house.

The pleasant evening unfolded, as they sat around the dining room table, enjoying chateaubriand, roasted red potatoes and asparagus. Dessert was the strawberry cheesecake that Billy Bingham had always loved.

By the time coffee and after-dinner drinks had been served and the goodbyes had been said, Kyle actually hated to see the evening end. But they would all gather again next month, when the Bingham clan came together to celebrate his grandmother's birthday.

Kyle had reconciled with the family he'd never

known, and he was about to embark upon a brand-new life with the woman he loved.

Did life get any better than this?

On the way home, Kyle glanced across the seat at Milla and smiled. "Your place or mine?"

"We'll have more privacy at your house." She flashed him a heated glance.

"You read my mind, honey."

"What about me?" Dylan asked. "Do I get to spend the night at your house, too?"

"We're a family," Kyle said. "And we're going to live together from now on."

"Cool!"

"But I think your mom and I had better start looking for a bigger house," Kyle added. They'd be outgrowing his little digs in no time at all.

"Your place is all right for now," Milla said. "Besides, if you're planning to move us to Boston—"

"I'm not," Kyle said. "While you and Myrtle were chatting about the first midwife in Merlyn County, I had a talk with Mari. There's room for me in the biomedical research facility she's developing."

"That's wonderful," Milla said. "If given a choice, I'd prefer to live in Merlyn County, but I'd move to Boston. As long as we can be together, it really doesn't matter."

She was right. All that mattered was being together. And home was wherever they could be a family.

"Speaking of living in Merlyn County," Kyle said.

"What do you think about us building a home near Ginman's Lake?"

"By the lake?" Dylan piped in. "That would be great. Then we could fish every single day."

Kyle laughed. "Well, that's two votes. Let's see what your mom has to say about it."

"As long as we're together, I'll be happy," Milla said. "But I do worry about my mother. It's going to be tough for her to make ends meet. I'll have to help her."

"I've got a better idea," Kyle said. "She can move into my place after we move out. I guarantee the rent will be affordable."

"She's kind of funny about taking charity."

"I know, but I'll offer her the same deal as my mother. Free rent in lieu of managing the place."

Milla brightened. "That just might appeal to her."

"I'm glad. And if I know my mom, they'll be friends as well as neighbors soon. They don't call Sally Woots the Bluebonnet Lane Welcoming Agency for nothing."

"Thank you for thinking about my mother. You're a good man, Kyle Bingham."

"I'm a *happy* man." Then he slid her a smile that promised he would love and cherish her forever.

*   *   *   *   *

Don't miss the continuation of
MERLYN COUNTY MIDWIVES
Delivering the miracle of life...and love!

FOREVER...AGAIN
By Maureen Child
Silhouette Special Edition #1604
Available April 2004

IN THE ENEMY'S ARMS
By Pamela Toth
Silhouette Special Edition #1610
Available May 2004

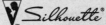

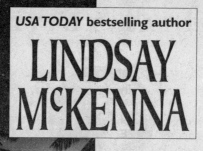

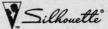

D.

Silhouette®

COMING NEXT MONTH

#1603 PRICELESS—Sherryl Woods
Million Dollar Destinies
Famed playboy Mack Carlton loved living the fast life—with even faster women—until he met Dr. Beth Browning. Beth's reserved, quiet ways brought out the deepest emotions in Mack, and soon had him wanting to believe in a slow and easy, forever kind of love. Could Mack convince Beth that his bachelor days were over?

#1604 FOREVER...AGAIN—Maureen Child
Merlyn County Midwives
You don't get a second chance at forever. That's what widower Ron Bingham believed. But, then, he hadn't counted on meeting PR whiz Lily Cunningham. The carefree beauty brought laughter and passion back into his life and made him wonder—was love even sweeter the second time around?

#1605 CATTLEMAN'S HEART—Lois Faye Dyer
Chaotic. That was the only way Rebecca Wallingford could describe her latest business trip. The superorganized accountant had been sent to oversee the expansion of a certain Jackson Rand's ranch. She'd never meant to get pulled into a whirlwind love affair with the rugged rancher...and she certainly hadn't planned on liking it!

#1606 THE SHEIK & THE PRINCESS IN WAITING—
Susan Mallery
Prince Reyhan had been commanded by his father, the King of Bahania, to marry as befit his position. There was just one tiny matter in the way: divorcing his estranged wife, Emma Kennedy. Seeing sweet Emma again brought back a powerful attraction...and something deeper. Could Reyhan choose duty over his heart's desire?

#1607 THE BEST OF BOTH WORLDS—Elissa Ambrose
Single. Unemployed. Pregnant. Becky Roth had a lot on her mind...not to mention having to break her pregnancy news to the father, Carter Prescott III. They'd shared one amazing night of passion. But small-town, small-*time* Becky was no match for Carter's blue-blooded background. The fact that she was in love with him didn't change a thing.

#1608 IN HER HUSBAND'S IMAGE—Vivienne Wallington
Someone was trying to sabotage Rachel Hammond's ranch. The widowed single mom's brother-in-law, Zack Hammond, arrived and offered to help find the culprit...but the sexy, rugged photographer stirred up unwelcome memories of their scandalous past encounter. Now it was just a matter of time before a shattering secret was revealed!

SSECNM0304R